About the Author

Sara Cottingham is a native of Colorado. She grew up spending most of her time outdoors, but she always had a book in her hand. Discovering her love for reading early, she pursued writing academically, earning her MFA in Creative Writing at Goddard College. Neon Girlfriend is her first published book. She has had short stories published in several journals, and she also worked at an indie publishing company learning the finer points of the publishing trade.

Neon Girlfriend

Sara Cottingham

Neon Girlfriend

Olympia Publishers
London

A CIP catalogue record for this title is
available from the British Library.

ISBN: 978-1-80074-769-2

This is a work of fiction.
Names, characters, places and incidents originate from the writer's
imagination. Any resemblance to actual persons, living or dead, is
purely coincidental.

First Published in 2023

Olympia Publishers
Tallis House
2 Tallis Street
London
EC4Y 0AB

Printed in Great Britain

Dedication

To my father, who I know will always be in my corner no matter what. To my mother, whose belief in me can never die. And finally, to my husband, who has always had faith in me, even when I didn't have confidence in myself.

Acknowledgements

There are many people who deserve a thank you for their endless support in watching my dream become a reality. To my small but mighty family: we have been through the gauntlet, but without your love and support I would not have had the courage to do this by myself. To the family I married into: my life has grown exponentially better since joining yours, and I grow more in love with you all as the years pass. To my friends who I met at college and beyond, you may have been a classmate that welcomed me into a group, or you may have been a teacher that I now consider a mentor and friend, but either way, your intellect and passion for writing continue to inspire me. Finally, to my fellow Air Force wives who I've met: you are my sisters. You have been there through the good and the bad, and no matter where we end up, our bond is something that miles cannot touch.

Chapter One

Reese worked as a security guard for the local parking garage, and in all his years he'd rarely seen anyone arrive before him. Indeed, never a police officer. The cop car blocked off the front entrance, its light whirling silently. They broke through the barely sun lit morning, ruining his usual routine. Reese's hand tightened on his tea thermos, and his feet slowed. He stayed where he was, across the street from the garage, under the shadow of an unlit bar sign. His thin, pale hair flopped back onto his forehead as he ran a hand through it before stepping off the curb and heading towards the garage.

The inside of the cement building glowed with artificial light, and he scanned the area, setting his things on the ground and out of the way. Reese spotted the officer walking towards him, head down, looking at the clipboard he carried, and he waved to get the man's attention. The officer's face was pulled into a frown as if two weights had been set at the corners of his mouth and allowed to dangle freely.

"What happened?" Reese asked quietly as the man approached him.

The cop eyed him with suspicion, and Reese quickly unzipped his worn sweatshirt to reveal his security badge and work clothes.

"Vehicle break-in," the officer said, glancing back down to his paperwork. "Looks like the guy left his car here overnight. I'll need to get your information since you're security."

11

"Is it all right if I go see if I can help? My office is right over there." Reese pointed to the small cinder block construction standing between the in- and outbound lanes of the garage. "I'll just set my things down and go check on the guy."

The officer shrugged and walked back towards his car. "Suit yourself. I'll be back in a minute to finish up my paperwork. There was a bunch of glass around the car, so if you have a broom, the area could use a sweep."

Reese quickly opened his office door and dropped his things onto the worn office chair before grabbing a broom and dustpan out of the gym-style lockers at the back of the office. Reese waved to the officer as he said something into his radio. The man waved him back towards the direction he'd come. Reese's shoes made a soft squeaking sound as he picked up his pace.

The garage was open twenty-four hours a day, but Reese was only required to be there during the operational hours of the building attached to it. Even as he searched for the car in question, he passed a sign stating the garage wasn't liable for any items stolen from the vehicles outside of working hours.

Reese finally spotted the tan car, and he ground his teeth together. Reese didn't know the man's name, but he always parked in the same spot every day—right near the sidewalk—and as far away as possible from any of the ancient security cameras still working on that level.

Reese watched the heavyset man waving his arms and talking into his cell phone. His hand tightened on his broomstick, and he considered simply turning around and leaving the man to deal with his own problems. As he stood there, the man finished up his phone call and turned to see Reese hovering.

"You think you'd know when something goes wrong in your garage, huh?"

Reese sighed out of his nose and shuffled towards the man.

"I try. The officer is finishing up some paperwork, but he should be right over. I'll start sweeping up the glass so that you don't cause a flat."

"I won't cause anything. You think this is my fault?" The man's face turned red, flushing to the tips of his ears, and Reese closed his eyes and counted to ten.

"I'm sorry. It obviously isn't your fault. I'll clean up here and get out of your way as soon as possible." Reese walked around to the other side of the car to look at the broken window, but the man followed him.

"You can't sweep this up. This is evidence."

Reese stuck his head into the car through the broken window and looked at the shattered glass on the backseat. "The officer asked me to sweep it up. It didn't sound like it was important." Reese didn't voice that he was trying to avoid someone else getting a flat at all costs. He pulled his head out of the opening and straightened, wiping any stray pieces of glass off of his shoulders and out of his hair.

Reese spotted the cop coming around the corner and relaxed as the heavyset man turned his attention back to the officer. He saw the cop's frown return as the driver rumbled towards him, but the man's cell phone started ringing again, giving the officer an excuse to meet Reese at the car. The cop handed Reese a clipboard with a blank form. Reese rested the broom on the cement side of the garage and took the offered pen.

"I just need your basic info," the officer said as he glanced back to the man. "I listed the stolen items and their value down below just in case you want to keep your eye out for them. My bet is they've already been pawned. Frankly, that guy couldn't have been more of an idiot."

Reese nodded along as he filled out his information. His hair flopped over his forehead and into his eyes, which he pushed out of the way. He glanced down at the list the cop provided and raised his eyebrows. *Garmin GPS. Value: $200. Why leave an expensive item like that out in view of everyone? Ray-Ban sunglasses and case: $275. I've never owned a pair of sunglasses worth more than $15. I need to ask for a raise. Woman's vintage ruby necklace: $600.* Reese stared at the price of the necklace for a long moment. *Why had the man left something like that in his car? Why not take it in with him? And what did the vintage part mean exactly?* Reese never cared much for antiques or jewelry, but he momentarily wondered if there was a significant difference between vintage and antique. Reese glanced at the man who was still talking furiously on his phone.

"Look, it's gone, all right? Yes, I checked the whole car. It's gone. Why would they take the damn GPS but leave the necklace? Even an idiot could tell the necklace was worth something. It weighs a ton. Well, we hadn't insured yet, had we? It wasn't my fault they broke into my car! This guard should have been watching. Hello?"

Reese glanced away and finished filling out his form.

"Look, do I have much more to do here?"

Reese glanced over at the cop as the officer answered. "I'd cover up the broken window somehow. Maybe with a plastic bag. The sooner you can get the glass replaced, the better."

The cop shrugged and glanced at Reese, who handed him back the clipboard with his provided information. The cop nodded to Reese before speaking to the heavyset man again.

"Other than that, I can offer you the warning to not leave valuables in your car. Neither the guard nor the garage is responsible. See if you can get the morning off to get the window fixed." The cop nodded to Reese before heading towards his car.

Reese stayed behind and began sweeping up the bits and pieces of broken glass just as other cars started arriving for the day. He waved to the drivers, and he got several greetings in return.

He walked out back to the large dumpsters and threw the broken bits of glass away before heading back towards his office. He didn't see the police officer or the fat man and released the breath he'd been holding when he finally reached his office and closed the door.

Filing his report of the theft forced Reese to start the aging computer. It turned on with a hot whir of motor and fan. Waiting the few minutes for the computer to boot up fully, he leaned back in his chair and took a sip of his now lukewarm tea. He wrinkled his nose before setting it aside.

He watched car after car stream into the garage, his foot jiggling anxiously as he counted them. The theft, and the arrival of the police, threw him off his morning routine. There was nothing more to be done on his end other than keep an eye out for the stolen items, but he knew the thief would be long gone. He'd never stolen anything himself, but he wasn't above admitting he'd been tempted to when cash was tight.

No, he'd never resorted to theft, but he had a girlfriend once who was a compulsive thief. He'd followed her patterns well enough. She'd bring something home and stuff it in a cardboard box in the hall closet for a week or so before taking it out of town to sell at a shop outside the local area. The thing that always bothered him about her stealing was she didn't do it for the money. It was simply a thrill for her.

The computer finished starting up, so he leaned forward and

reached into one of the desk drawers to pull out a pair of reader glasses. Still squinting slightly because the lens power wasn't entirely accurate, he pecked out the form using his pointer fingers. He read over the report before printing out two copies, one to be filed in his office and the other to be sent upstairs to the head of security within the building.

Content with his work for the morning, Reese turned around in his office chair, one he'd saved from the dump pile because the only thing wrong with it was a small tear in the seat, and took a look at his office. Several boxes he needed to break down and take out to the dumpster stood at the back of the narrow office. The door to the office sat to his right, and next to that was a set of fold-up chairs stacked neatly and covered in a fine layer of dust.

His most prized possession hung just above the light switch. It was a certificate of excellence his boss awarded him the night the old man retired and when Reese took over all the responsibilities of the garage. "People wouldn't know what to do with themselves if you weren't around, Reese." Bill, his boss, might have been a bit too far gone on the punch, and his words slightly slurred, but Reese knew he was being honest. "They might not say anything, but I sure appreciate it." It wasn't an official certificate since it had just been the two of them up until that point. Bill printed it off the office printer and tacked it to the wall with thumbtacks. Reese had since taken down and framed it, but it still read Bill's retirement year of 1998, almost six years ago.

Hours later, Reese struggled to roll the spare wheel into place on the flat tire he was fixing. The sunset lit the floor of the garage orange and warmed his back. The woman who asked for his help tapped her foot as he straightened to grab the wrench to put the bolts back in place.

Reese had hoped he could get off work tonight without anyone needing his help, but he'd always given support to those who asked. His arms ached as he tightened the nuts into place, but he finished and packed up the rest of the equipment into the back of the woman's car. The woman rounded the back just as Reese shut the trunk and offered him a hurried thank you before getting into the driver's seat to start the car.

Reese coughed as the exhaust kicked back into his face. Waving the fumes away, he saw the woman already heading towards the exit of the garage. Reese ran a hand through his hair, offering himself a thank you for a job well done before heading towards the stairwell leading to his office.

Most people who worked for the manufacturing company attached to the garage arrived just before nine a.m. and left before five. He gathered up the dustpan and broom he'd abandoned by the office when the woman requested help with her tire and began his nightly ritual of sweeping the area around his office. He could have blamed the flat tire on this morning's break-in, but the woman parked up on the third floor, and Reese knew he'd swept the area clean that morning. Someone always needed a flat fixed or windshield wiper fluid topped off, and most days he was happy to help.

He gathered his dustpan and headed back towards the dumpsters to throw the litter away. The flashing light of the dive bar across the street caught his eyes, and his feet slowed as he took in the dancing lady on the sign.

Rouge Palace had been there as long as he could remember. The building hadn't aged well; its paint long since worn off, the parking lot constantly littered with trash, and yet, Reese had always wanted to visit. It was consistently frequented by the men who worked in the adjoining building, often telling their wives they had to work until six so they could spend some time drinking with the girls. The neon lady atop the sign kicked her feet back and forth, pulling Reese in, making him want to drop everything to belong to her, but he resisted and started walking again.

It was a windy, warm night at the end of summer, and as he rounded the corner of the building towards the dumpster, he saw two men from the company smoking cigarettes underneath a street lamp.

"He just hangs around the garage all day. What does he do? Sweeps and waves to you when you drive by. That's a pathetic life."

Reese adjusted the dustpan in his hand and hung back. The heavyset man chuckled at what he'd just said. It was the same man from this morning, and Reese felt his back stiffen at the accusation, but the other man spoke up, his voice crimped with irritation.

"He may be a loner, but I know he's helped you a time or two." The smoke from their cigarettes drifted towards the neighboring foreclosed buildings.

The heavyset man stamped out his cigarette and coughed. "Yeah, whatever. That guy just doesn't look like he belongs anywhere, so instead, he loiters around the garage, overly eager to help." He stretched, the motion pushing his rotund belly against the buttons of his shirt. "Let's head over to Rouge Palace for a bit. I need a drink and a pretty girl to give me attention. Being home has been crappy with my mother-in-law moving in. And after the break-in, I deserve a beer."

The other man shook his head, taking a step away from the other man and crushing his own smoke. "I have to get home. You have fun, Lester." The man who defended Reese hurried away quickly without looking back.

Looking at the man, Reese could say he would never help him again. Reese waited a moment before emerging from the shadows. He picked up both discarded cigarette wrappers and dropped them to rest in the already full dustpan. Reese didn't make a habit of listening in on other people's conversations, but he was vain enough to admit he wanted to know what they thought of him. He turned away, his shoulders slumping.

He upended the contents of the dustbin into the dumpster and stood there, hand on the lid for a few moments, staring out across the street to the bar.

Reese hurried back to the office, filled with a sudden inspiration to make something good come from this hectic day. Reese had always wanted to visit Rouge Palace. He opened the small locker at the back of his office and adjusted his appearance in the small mirror. Reese was simply androgynous: a thin, gawkish man whose long fingers always seemed to be reaching for something even as he tried to keep the rest of himself inconspicuous. His gray-white hair, blue eyes, and pale complexion meant he blended in with the walls of the garage. In truth, he'd worked there for so long and so diligently that he'd begun to resemble the concrete and cinder block construction. Still, the comments Lester made had Reese clenching his fists and glaring at his pale reflection.

He gathered his keys and wallet before locking up for the night. Despite the warm evening, Reese still slipped into his jacket. Part habit and part comfort, he was overly warm by the time he crossed the street and found himself at the front doors of Rouge Palace. Sweat beaded on his back, and he felt pinpricks of a very different, nervous sweat growing underneath his armpits.

He reached forward and grasped the handle, cold in his hand and worn smooth. He briefly wondered what Lester's face would look like when he saw Reese sitting at the bar.

The brightness of the sign vanished as Reese plunged inside the near darkness. Dancers twisted and dipped on poles and along the stage. A bar back-lit with neon orange lights highlighted rows of alcohol. The bartender moved in flashes and spurts as he shifted from customer to customer. Customer's faces were caught in a half-light; some part of them wanted to move in shadows while another part relished the anonymity. People crushed together at the bar and along the booth circling the stage. Well-dressed men in suits dominated the booths while men in grease-stained overalls and baseball caps crowded the bar.

The tables were covered in drinks and crumpled up napkins. Plates of bar food were passed around on trays that the hostesses held well above their heads even as they danced away from the seeking hands of the customers. The smell of the place was not what Reese had imagined. It was a strange mixture of smoke and orange blossoms. A few quick breaths acclimated him to the slightly dusty air. He believed he could see the air he took into himself as a stream of smoke punctuated by bright fissures of orange, and he felt uplifted as his lungs filled.

Someone tapped his shoulder from behind, and he jerked around. Reese stared at the man's chin and tipped his head up to take in the man who came in after him. Under a black shirt, a smattering of tattoos covered the bands of muscle down the length of the man's arms. He rolled his eyes and quickly stepped around Reese, heading towards the bar. Reese ground his teeth, unable to make the same move, and sighed when he saw the man talking comfortably with one of the women serving drinks from trays.

The lights dimmed everywhere except for the bar and the main stage. The majority of the people hushed, and Reese's scalp prickled with sweat. He was rooted to the spot; the sudden stillness of the room forced him to remain by the door. He stepped back, his hand reaching for the handle as he regretted his decision to come in in the first place. His mouth felt like scratchy cotton, his tongue stuck to the roof of his mouth, and he glanced over to the bar and myriad of drinks.

Overhead, speakers crackled to life, and a husky female voice came on.

"Ladies and gentlemen, please join me in welcoming our main performance tonight. She needs no introduction besides her name. Give a warm Rouge Palace welcome to Lady Rouge herself!" A rowdy booth of young men cheered wildly, drawing the ire of the other patrons, but everyone turned back to their drinks in a matter of moments.

Reese swallowed hard and took a hesitant step away from his post at the door, but sound blared from the speakers, locking him in place. A strange combination of southern twangy-rock mixed with light touches of classical made him shake his head and rub his ears.

A woman appeared on stage, and Reese felt the need for a drink grow stronger than ever. His desire to find Lester and shove his appearance in the other man's face vanished in a haze of cigarette smoke as he watched Lady Rouge come up to the front of the stage to begin her dance. She was curvy, but not overweight. She had the type of build that never appeared in magazine spreads, and he found it endearing. She wore a blood orange costume like she'd been born to wear it, and the color made her dark skin glow. But her movements seemed to lack the fluidity he expected. She contradicted his instant mental image of a woman with a name like "Lady Rouge," but she seemed to fit the dissonant music more than the setting. All the lights changed from their assorted colors to just a swathe of red, washing out her skin tone and making her look ashen. He squinted at her face, but she turned before he could fully see it. Being lit from below reminded Reese of the times he held a flashlight under his face in the dark to make himself look like a skeleton.

As she danced for the customers along the opposite side of the stage from the bar, Reese felt like he could finally make a break for the empty bar seat he'd spotted. He lurched forward, and his foot caught on the outstretched shoe of another patron, causing his eyes to widen and his stomach to lurch as he crashed into one of the girls carrying a round of drinks. The glasses cascaded in a wave across the floor, and the girl's cursing was loud, drawing the stares from the bartender and customers, but also Lady Rouge. He turned to see her gaze locked on him. Her eyes were morning fog gray. He scrambled up, dashing past the waitress already cleaning up the plastic cups, and saw another girl heading over with towels. He slid into the open seat at the bar and turned his face towards the wall of bottles, so no one would see his flushed face.

The condensation on his neighboring customer's glass drove Reese mad with thirst, but he waited for his face to cool before drawing any more attention. He decided he'd count to five and then call out to the bartender. Reese didn't know how many times he'd counted to five and opened his mouth, but the words kept getting stuck on the dry cotton of his mouth. Hunched and frowning, he sat there and watched as the bartender helped the last of the straggling guests order their liquor.

"You gonna order something, pal?"

Reese blinked up to see the bartender standing in front of him. The man raised his eyebrows, and Reese fumbled for the menu.

"Ah, yes, please, sorry. I, uh, would like a glass of water and your strongest whiskey."

The man sized him up. "We only have one type of whiskey, and I gotta be honest, it isn't great."

"That's fine. Can you mix it, then? An Old Fashioned?"

After checking his ID, the bartender filled a glass of water and set it down on the bar. Reese fell on it and drank half the glass in just a few gulps. The water hit his empty stomach and sloshed violently. The bartender set a glass of amber-colored liquid on the bar. Reese hadn't seen the drink since his father passed away several years prior, and the bartender had indeed done a better job at presentation than his father when he'd made them at home.

"Thanks."

Reese picked up the glass and sniffed at the liquid. The smell of alcohol and woodsy heather hit him full force. He took a small sip and tried not to choke. The sips he'd stolen from his father's mix over the years had gotten weaker and weaker, so the full force of a properly made drink was almost overwhelming. He gingerly set the glass down and took a sip of water. The water was icy cold and bland and swirled the remaining whiskey around in his mouth until his brain felt muddled.

He rotated the glass on the counter and watched the reflections of the dancers in the amber liquid. Lady Rouge had long since left the stage, and he kept watching out of the corner of his eye to see if he could spot her. She was the neon lady on the sign come to life. He swirled the drink in the glass and took

23

another sip. It wasn't nearly as potent this time around, and he glanced at the clock behind the bar, wondering how long he'd been sitting there.

The bartender came up to him and tapped the edge of his drink with his knuckle.

"You ever gonna finish that?"

The man's face was heavily wrinkled and deeply tanned. The wrinkles added age to his face, making him look over fifty, but he couldn't be more than forty. The man's shirt was a faded black, with holes in the collar that came from use. He was too old to be playing into the emerging trend of everything being distressed to look more grunge. The muscles in the man's arms were thick, and Reese had watched him moving boxes of alcohol behind the bar and taking the trash out the side door all evening.

Reese nodded quickly and finished off the rest of his drink. Relaxed in his current position by the wall, Reese took a moment to study the well-polished wood of the bar. The numerous patrons had smoothed over the scratches and nicks over the years. Each blemish countered by a sweep of a hand, the wood absorbing sweat and alcohol alike. Someone had polished it relatively recently, so the shine was still brilliant in the parts of the bar that saw less use, and in those spots, he could see a clear reflection of the ceiling and lighting above.

He picked up his glass, which up until this point had been resting on the bar, and placed it on the provided coaster. He felt a bit ashamed he hadn't used it up until then and absentmindedly reached a hand towards the stack of napkins to clean up the condensation left by his glass.

A hand came into view, holding one of the napkins, and he glanced up to say thank you before staring dumbly at the person. He recognized her instantly as Lady Rouge, out of costume and wonderfully close to him. He took the napkin and muttered a thank you, watching her reflection in the bar.

She sighed and stretched her neck.

"Christ, tonight was boring. Gimme a mule, would you?"

The bartender patted her hand and set a glass in front of her. Reese had watched him mixing it before she'd reached the bar. It seemed that Lady Rouge habitually visited the bar after her shift and that made Reese like her even more.

"You're a saint."

"Nah, but I got to take care of my girl, don't I?" The bartender went about wiping down the countertops.

Remnants of thick stage makeup were still apparent around her eyes where the black and red liner was stuck to the outer corners. Her skin looked tired, as if she spent too much time trying to make herself look good with paints and colors and not enough time taking care of her body. Her hair was laboriously straightened and pulled back in a clip. Now that she was only a few feet from him, Reese saw that she struck a strange contrast with herself. Her outward appearance pointed to being worn down. With her tired skin and a ratty sweatshirt, Reese might have thought life had taken its best swing at her and won, but her voice and eyes gave him another picture. Her voice possessed a low timbre, but it held none of the fatigue that lined the rest of her body. Her eyes were large, or perhaps the neon lights made them appear that way, but the gray color seemed to reflect whatever she was looking at, and Reese wondered if anyone would ever be able to lie to Lady Rouge. He couldn't imagine looking at those eyes and being anything other than honest.

She glanced at him and smiled. There was a hint of warmth there, but it was mostly a searching smile. Reese guessed she was trying to figure out what he was doing here so late, and he hoped he didn't come off as lecherous.

"D'ya see my dance?" She leaned her head against her hand and swirled her drink. She bit the corner of her lip and chewed at the flaky skin.

Reese nodded and took a sip of his drink. He wrapped his hands around the glass and tried to convince his throat to open up so he could speak to her.

"D'ya like it?"

Reese nodded again as the bartender snorted. "You've been dancing that same routine for how long? I'm sure he could dance your set for you with his eyes closed."

Lady Rouge swatted at him. "You shouldn't be rude to a lady."

Reese watched their exchange wanting to be part of their banter. He could tell they were close friends; the bartender's words were nothing more than a joke. Her eyes crinkled in the corners as she smiled, and Reese knew it was a genuine smile, not like the one she gave him. They continued to talk. The current situation didn't surprise Reese, but he found it did bother him. Lady Rouge wouldn't turn and look at him again, and he desperately wanted to tell her how much he enjoyed seeing her dance; although, he preferred her in her sweatshirt, talking at the bar.

"I—I did like your dance." He felt as if he shouted this, but he was forced to say it twice at ever-increasing volume until she turned her head.

"Aw, thanks. What's your name?"

Her eyes locked onto his, and he fought against his habit of lowering his eyes to his hands.

"Reese."

"Reese? My name's Millie Rae, but most people don't say the second half, so Millie's fine."

"I think I like Millie Rae more."

She leaned back a bit in her chair and stared at him for a moment before returning to her drink.

"So, what brought you in tonight, Reese?"

26

Reese fiddled with the edge of his jacket and glanced around the bar.

"Someone from work was supposed to be here. I thought I'd see if I could say hello, but I don't think he showed."

Millie Rae hummed and turned back to him. She tapped her nails on the bar.

"Is this person a friend?"

Reese shook his head. "No. More an annoyance."

Millie Rae smiled at him.

"So, you thought you'd come and what?" She spread her arms wide. "Out drink him in this fine establishment?"

Reese frowned and finished his drink. "Something like that."

She laughed. It was a deep laugh that came from her belly. Reese felt his face grow warm, and he pushed away from the bar, but Millie Rae's hand clamped down on his.

"I'm sorry. Truly, I wasn't laughing at you. Well, maybe a little, but you look like a strong wind could blow you over."

She released his hand raised her hand for two more drinks.

Reese felt an embarrassed grin form, and he pulled himself back up to the bar.

"The guy probably outweighs me by a hundred pounds."

Millie Rae laughed again, and Reese joined her as the absurdity of his plan became more real. The bartender came up and gave Reese his check. Reese handed him the cash and threw the change in the tip jar.

"Do you think if I keep coming around, you'll keep visiting with me, Millie Rae?"

"You know, Reese, I think I just might."

Chapter Two

A week later, Reese walked up the trembling steps to his apartment — number six. The paint was peeling off the door, and the original plastic six had long since fallen off, leaving only the shadow imprint behind. It had been his parent's apartment when his father worked two jobs nearby, and his mother was a waitress. Both his parents passed away several years ago, but after having been there so long, they'd struck a deal with the manager. An under-the-table agreement meant their rent was cheaper than the newer tenants. Reese was entitled to the same deal so long as he didn't move. The door never opened easily, and he shoved against it to get in. He flicked the light on, closed the door and hung up his hoodie. Same as he'd always done. He rolled his neck and headed for the kitchen to get a drink when a knock came from his door. He considered not answering it for a moment, but the knock sounded again.

The super stood on his doorstep. The skeletal man always seemed to wear clothes that accentuated his bony frame. The man's yellowed teeth showed through the thin mouth as he grinned at Reese. "You owe me your rent."

Reese held his breath as the scent of alcohol drifted close to his nose. He waited a moment before replying. "I got paid today, but I didn't have time to go to the ATM. Can you wait until tomorrow? I can put it underneath your door." Reese's hand tightened on the door as the man chewed on the inside of his cheek.

"Rent's gone up, and I need it now."

"What do you mean the rent has gone up?" Reese stepped back, rejecting the statement.

The man stepped through the doorway and wrenched the door shut, closing them both inside. He turned back to Reese and squinted up at him. "You heard me. New apartment complex is going up a couple of blocks from here. Fancy people moving in. I gotta fix this place up if I'm going to keep my tenants, and to do that, I gotta raise my prices. So, your rent is going up." Reese shook his head, trying to step around the man, but he reached out and pushed Reese back towards the living room.

"You can't do that," Reese said. "You should have to give notice of that sort of thing."

"Maybe," the man grinned, showing his missing front tooth. "Maybe I do for people who have a lease, but you're here on the goodness of my heart, and as such, I didn't think a lease would be necessary. So, rent is going up. You pay, or you leave. Ain't my problem." The man turned toward the door.

"Wait," Reese said. "Just give me some time." Reese couldn't hide the plaintive rise in his voice. His mouth was sour with the fact he had to beg to stay in this place. "I wouldn't have anywhere else to go."

"Don't I know it," the man said, pushing his glasses back up the bridge of his nose. He left, slamming the door behind him. The mugs hanging on their pegs in the kitchen jangled.

Reese ran a face down his hand and looked around the tiny apartment he had called home his entire life. The kitchen with its peeling wallpaper was to his left, and the small living/dining room with its yellowed sofa and faulty T.V. occupied most of the square footage. The bathroom was small, and he'd left a damp towel on the floor from this morning's shower.

He picked it up and hung it on the towel rod, wrinkling his nose at the mildew smell wafting from the towel, irritated he'd skipped the coin wash over the weekend. He sat on his bed and glanced out the window. His window was his favorite part of the apartment because of its view. When he stepped up to the glass, pressing his cheek against the cool pane, and looked down the street, he saw the pink lady kicking her legs back and forth on the sign. Sometimes the light from her glow would be strong enough that it would flash off the walls of his bedroom as he fell asleep.

Reese returned to Rouge Palace the next night. He'd never been one to drink away his problems, but he'd never been threatened with eviction before. He pushed his way into Rouge Palace without the hesitancy of the first time and waded past the people crowded around the dance floor. It didn't matter if he spent all the cash in his wallet. He rarely looked forward to returning to his lonely apartment, but being there now felt even more constricting under the threatening gaze of his landlord. He slid in between two other customers and waved down the bartender.

"Hey Reese," the man said as he came over, glass in hand, as he cleaned it with a rag. "What can I get you?"

"I'd have water and a beer."

The man nodded and glanced back down the row of taps along the front of the bar. "We got light or dark."

"Light."

The man nodded and left Reese. Reese reached out and took several napkins from the nearby stack and placed them in front of himself. He glanced briefly to the stage and saw two women but felt nothing for them. It was almost as though he were a set of eyes and nothing more. He saw the images, but the emotional reaction he should have had simply wasn't there.

There was the storm of people around him: whirling, sporadic, and loud; he was the center: quiet, impassive, and uninterested. He pressed the heels of his palms into the sockets of his eyes until they hurt before opening them to see the red spots flickering along his vision.

The bartender came back with his drink and set it in front of him. Reese nodded at the man, who hovered momentarily, frowning, before directing his attention to another patron. Reese rotated his beer bottle around, watching the liquid before putting it to his lips and finishing half in several gulps. The frigidness of the beer shocked his brain back to functioning, his situation suddenly very jagged and real. He took another sip of his beer, his hand shaking. He would be out on the streets unless he found an equally morally corrupt landlord willing to do an under-the-table deal.

Reese drank the other half of his beer quickly. The bartender swung by and picked up the glass. Reese held out his hand and asked for another before the man got any farther down the bar. Reese looked around at the people walking upstairs to the private rooms with his second beer in hand. The whole top level of the bar was hidden in shadow and tucked back from the railing where several people milled about. He turned to ask the bartender about the private rooms but chewed on his words before swallowing them back down again.

He glanced at his watch, wondering if Millie Rae had already done her dance, but seeing her wouldn't help the mood he was in. He ran his hands through his hair and scratched his neck. The bartender picked up a load of trash and carried it out the side exit, the heavy bang of the closing door only barely audible over the music. He finished his second beer and left cash on the bar, tucking it underneath his glass. Intent on letting the bartender know he'd paid for his drinks just in case someone thought to slip the cash in their pocket, he quickly went out the side door.

The warm, humid weather hit him in the lungs as he took a breath. The side alley of the bar was dingy and stunk of the industrial size trash bins to his left. He stepped down onto the street as he shoved his hands in his pockets. He had an early morning, but he lingered a moment by the door of the bar.

The bartender came into view from his left, a black bag still in his hand, and he paused when he saw Reese.

"You shouldn't be back here," he said, setting the bag down momentarily as he turned to stare at Reese.

"I wanted to let you know I paid my tab. I thought it was just another exit."

The man shook his head and pointed to the alley exit behind Reese's shoulder. "That's the way out. I don't want to see you back here again." He lifted the bag off the ground and waited until Reese made his move.

Reese turned to go, embarrassment coloring the back of his neck, and his shoes splashed through the puddles as he hurried towards the alleyway opening. He paused when he heard a crash from the direction of the garbage bins accompanied by a female's raised voice. He hesitated but quickly moved back towards the garbage bins, pulling his hands out of his pockets as he went.

As he drew closer, Reese heard the woman's voice again.

"Listen, I don't pay you to skim off the top of my supply. My boys won't double-cross me, so you better have an explanation. The girls can be complimentary for all I care, but customers sure as hell better pay for my product." The woman's voice was sharp, and as Reese rounded the corner of the trash bin, he saw that she was faced away from him, staring up at the bartender.

Reese stayed partially hidden in the shadow of the garbage bin and waited.

"Listen, Naomi," the bartender began, "I'm not skimming. Your boys are good, and they always pay for their drinks fair and square. I can't say if something is happening in the private rooms with the guys and the dancers. That's the girl's fault, not mine."

The woman stepped closer to the bartender, and Reese was shocked to see the large man take a step back and hold up his hands.

"Honest. I'll talk to the girls, all right? You brought that new girl in, right? I can talk to her about how the dealings are supposed to work."

Reese turned around; his movements were jerky as he tried to leave without either party knowing he'd heard them. As he rounded the corner into the alleyway, his foot caught on the edge of a discarded trash bag, sending him sprawling in the filthy water of the alleyway. His hands dug into the loose dirt on the ground as he quickly tried to pick himself up, but rough hands suddenly grabbed him from the back of his shirt, lifting him into the air. He slammed into the trash bin face first, the stench almost making him retch.

"Turn him around," the woman's voice ordered.

He blinked his eyes, trying to clear the water and grit from them. The bartender held Reese by the front of his shirt as the woman walked closer. She was alarmingly thin, the skin of her face stretched taught over angular cheekbones. Her hair was dark and pulled back into a bun at the base of her neck.

"You aren't supposed to be back here," she said. Her voice was smooth, deceptively soft. "Is he a regular?"

"I'm not," Reese answered before the bartender could. "I won't come back, I swear. I didn't even like any of your girls."

33

"He's soft on Millie Rae," the bartender said.

The woman crossed her arms and studied Reese for a few moments. Reese glanced towards the alleyway opening, praying someone would walk by and see what was happening.

"Millie's been a thorn in my side for years," the woman ground out. She tapped her finger against her lip as she stared at Reese. "He's soft on her, you say? I wonder how quiet you'd stay to keep her safe."

Reese turned back to her and thrashed his head from side to side. "I'm not, I swear. I won't come back. Please, just let me go."

The woman reached out and snagged Reese's chin in her grasp, forcing his head still so she could stare at his face. He kept his eyes down. "Either way, you've made a mistake," he said.

"No, I haven't." She released his chin, her sharp nails catching the side of his face and scratching his cheek. "You're the security guard for the garage next door."

Reese fixed his gaze on her again, hoping to see something in her he recognized.

"No, I doubt you'd recognize me. I make sure other people handle my business over there." She tapped her nail against her mouth as she looked at him. "Regardless, I'm sure you'll see me around now." She took a step back and sighed.

"Let him go, Mike. He heard us, but there isn't much we can do about it here."

"I'll forget everything I heard," Reese said as Mike released the front of his shirt. He edged to the side, desperate to get away from both of them.

The woman, Naomi, glanced at him and smiled. It pulled at her mouth, a gash opening wide in her face. "I don't doubt you'll try, but know this: I'll be watching you." She turned back to Mike and waved her hand at Reese. "Have a nice night."

Reese turned from the alleyway and hurried home, only letting out the breath he'd been holding once the door to his apartment closed.

Reese fumbled for the keys to his office the next morning and glanced at the clock through his office windows. After tossing and turning in a clammy ball half the night, he'd finally fallen asleep and forgot to set his alarm. He rubbed his forehead where a headache rested, and his hands shook as he struggled to unlock the door to the security office.

None of the businesses' employees ever arrived before they were required, but Reese always liked to feel settled before they got there. Their influx of gas fumes and under-the-breath grumbling about the morning's traffic jam always made him feel jittery.

He set a thermos of English Breakfast tea on the desk and noticed the paperwork from the robbery still sitting on his desk. There wasn't anything more to be done about the break-in, so after setting his tea down on the desk, he picked the papers up and tucked them into a file folder.

He took a seat in his chair before immediately standing back up again and pacing to the door. He opened it, staring outside at the empty parking spaces for a few moments before shutting himself inside the office once more.

From his window, he could see the far corner of Rouge Palace. He hardly glanced at the people who began trickling in for work. The woman last night took up too much of his focus. He was sure he'd never seen her before, but she knew him. Knew that he worked here.

Sweat beaded under his armpits at the thought that she could be watching him now. He stood up again and walked to the back of his office, carrying his thermos. He dug through the organized piles of unwanted goods back there until he pulled out a dented and scratched clipboard. He brought it to his desk and clipped some printer paper onto it. He knew her name was Naomi, or at least he thought it was. She could have lied. He wrote down her name with a question mark.

He unscrewed the top to his thermos and watched through the security monitor as the parking garage began to swell with mid-priced sedans. From his vantage point at his desk, he could not see anything of Rouge Palace except the delicate toes of the dancer. The sign was off, but it was apparent the dancer had too many legs in the daylight. At night her legs flashed, so it appeared that one of her feet was kicking, but in the glare of light, Reese could see the neon dancer sported one extra calf and foot.

He never needed to walk the garage after the cars came in, but he always took his thermos with him, and it had become a bit of a ritual to calm him from the onslaught of the morning's rush. His walk of the garage and his maintenance of the stairs leading to the upper floors had become his little ritual. His job was to maintain the garage; his responsibility was to keep the cars protected without incident until their owners returned. There were three flights of the garage, and he always took the stairs. People still left trash in the stairwell, and it bothered him that people always felt they could freely litter in his place of work. He never went into their offices and dumped all of his shredded documents on their desks, but no matter.

He rested his thermos on the edge of the concrete wall on the top level and ground his teeth. He finished his walk around the garage, always ending on the top. It was in perfect view of Rouge

Palace, and he felt the heat rise up the back of his neck.

In the day, he expected himself to be less fearful of the dark alleyway where he'd been threatened last night, but the building still cast a long shadow. Even with his fear, he was drawn to the three-legged siren on the board. He told himself he wouldn't be going back anytime soon. Drugs and gangs were a common enough occurrence in the area, one reason he'd always kept his head down, but it seems that his number had been pulled. He hoped staying away from the bar for a while would lessen the woman's interest in him. He couldn't deny that he wanted to be around Millie Rae more. Thinking of her, he felt his blush rise to cover his whole head. He'd had crushes before. This felt similar, but deeper, more comforting. Almost as if the attraction he felt now would fade away, leaving behind something stronger.

Several weeks passed with little response from the police about the theft in the garage. Reese might have let it go, but Lester continued to make comments and remarks about him to others within earshot, like trash piling up. Reese was taking bags out to the dumpster when two police officers drove up and got out of their car. He frowned, having just done a lap of the garage. Everything had been quiet. He paused before setting the bag down, wiping his hands off on his slacks, and walking over to them.

He saw Lester coming over to them from the corner of his eye and almost rolled his eyes when he saw the man still refused to change his parking spot. Reese might not have bothered seeing what the issue was since he was so close to being done with his day, but he knew better than to be rude.

"Can I help you, officers?" The men glanced at Lester's approaching form before turning to Reese. One of the men had a mustache that grew long over his mouth. The other looked barely out of high school and stood slightly behind the older man. The man with the mustache turned and nodded to the younger one, who fumbled with his breast pocket for a moment before finally undoing the button and pulling out a piece of paper.

"We got a request for a follow-up on a burglary that happened here last week." The younger officer's voice was astonishingly deep, contrasting sharply with his lanky frame. He quickly handed Reese the piece of paper. "My name is Officer Stevens, and my superior is Officer Cummings. Were you the gentleman who made the call?"

Reese shook his head and was about to answer when Lester's huffing breath finally reached their ears. The three of them turned and surveyed the man as he made the last few paces to stand with them.

His face was blister red, and his breath wheezed thinly as he tried to take several deep breaths before speaking. "I called you," he said. He grabbed the paper from Reese's hand and looked it over. "This is just a copy of the original report that was filed."

The younger officer coughed slightly and nodded. "Yes, well, the department isn't confident that we can help you any further. Unless you have an idea of who might have taken your things, we have no leads."

Lester turned towards the young man, and Reese felt a bubble of pity rise in his stomach as the younger man seemed suddenly doubtful about drawing Lester's attention.

"No leads?" Lester took a step towards Stevens, and Reese swore the young officer took a slight step behind Officer Cummings. "It's your job to find the leads, not my job to tell you where to look."

Officer Cummings raised his hand, blocking Lester's

advance towards the younger officer. "Mr. Lester, there isn't much we can do at this point, and it says there right on the report that the responding officer gave the same advice. Now, if you are bent on having the items returned to you, I can suggest hiring a private investigator. I know of several who know the area well. They would be able to devote their time to finding your lost items. The police force does not have the workforce to dedicate time to this specific task."

It sounded rehearsed, but it had the desired effect of getting Lester to back down. He huffed into Officer Cummings face, and Reese gave the older man credit; he merely reached into his breast pocket and pulled forth a list of names, which he handed to Lester. "This is a list of private investigators that I have worked with in the past, and I can vouch for their professionalism."

He turned to Reese. "If Mr. Lester chooses to move forward with this, whichever person he chooses will answer to him, but because the incident happened in a company-run area, it might be good to acquaint yourself with the coming and goings of the P.I. They might want to speak with you." Officer Cummings nodded to Reese by way of goodbye, and shook hands with a now stoic Lester before turning his still quivering shadow around and taking them both back to the police car.

Reese glanced over to Lester, but he was solely focused on the names on the piece of paper. Reese said nothing and returned to his job. He felt mildly guilty at not saying goodnight to Lester, but good manners felt almost like a waste on the man.

He found an envelope dropped into his small office mailbox the following day. He set his mug down and took a seat before opening the letter.

Lester wasted no time. He'd hired a P.I. named Stanley to

look into his stolen items. The paperwork continued to say that Reese should expect Stanley to stop by any day the following week to review the paperwork Reese filed with the garage. Lester never gave up. Was it his pride, or were the items more important than what they seemed? He'd listed the price of the jewelry on the original report, a significant amount, but to hire a private investigator to look into it? It seemed insane. Surely, he'd pay the investigator more than the necklace was worth.

Reese crumpled the paper and threw it in the trashcan before moving to turn on the computers for the morning. The man didn't know when to quit, so let him spend his money. Reese had nothing to hide.

Chapter Three

A large truck was blocking the entrance to the garage when Reese arrived several mornings later. A nondescript silver, the vehicle didn't have a blemish, and the expensive-looking headache rack and toolbox told Reese that whoever drove the truck took a lot of pride in the vehicle. He walked around the tail of the truck, glancing at his watch, trying to guess how long it would take for him to convince the driver to move his vehicle. Reese didn't need a car since he could walk to work, and public transportation took him everywhere else, but he imagined that the man felt the same about his truck as Reese did about his garage. Reese heard a murmuring of voices by the driver's side door as the noise of the street faded behind him. Wondering what sort of dispute he would find, he leaned his head around the truck to see a man's back and two of the cleaning ladies who worked in the building talking to him animatedly.

He towered over both women, and their necks were bent at an awkward angle as they tried to maintain eye contact. The opened hood of a car to his right caught Reese's attention, and he recognized it as one of the cleaning lady's cars. They often carpooled together, so he couldn't be sure as to which owned this particular vehicle. Not a dispute. A nice man offering help.

Reese stepped forward and straightened his shoulders, feeling almost protective of the two women, although he could see the man meant them no harm.

"Is there something I can help you both with?"

The women quickly shook their heads as the man turned around and looked at Reese. The man was astonishingly tall, beyond the point that it was attractive, and Reese wondered how often it was the first thing he probably heard when he was introduced to a new person. Reese guessed him at around six foot six. He wasn't scrawny, either, this man who had endeared himself so thoroughly to these two women. He was built in a way that Reese wondered how many hours a day he spent at the gym. Even underneath the button-down shirt and slacks, Reese saw that his clothes fit snugly around the corded muscle. Reese felt himself shrink in proximity to this man. He was everything that Reese would never be.

Reese finished studying the man before turning back to the woman and listened as she pulled him over to her car and pointed at the battery. Reese leaned his head inside and saw that the positive and negative posts had become corroded.

"I went ahead and unplugged the battery, but I didn't have anything to clean them off," the man said behind him. He sounded almost apologetic, like he'd expected more of himself regarding his impromptu rescue.

Reese straightened and smiled at the two women.

"I can fix this. It just needs to be cleaned. Do you have a few minutes while I grab what I need?"

They shrugged, having nowhere else to go, and opened the back door of the car to set their bags inside while they waited. Reese turned to the man, who was waiting by the hood of his truck.

"I think we're all set here," Reese said.

The man nodded but jingled his keys in his hand and remained standing where he was.

"I think I'm supposed to be meeting someone here. My name

is Stanley. I'm the P.I. that Mr. Lester hired."

Reese sighed. "You'll be meeting me. My name is Reese, but I need you to move your truck. You're blocking the entrance. People will be arriving soon." Reese pointed to a section of parking spaces that had long been painted over with hashed yellow lines. "Just park there. I don't have enough space to have you taking one of the regular spots. Unless you want to park on the roof and walk back down." Reese was almost hoping Stanley would find the spot too tight and be forced to walk, giving him time to take a breath while he dealt with the car, but Stanley eyed the space and nodded. He quickly got in his truck, starting the loud engine, while Reese jogged over to his office and opened it up to get the supplies he needed.

Cleaning off the battery and plugging the cables back on took only a few minutes, but his hands were filthy after. He offered a smile to the lady, who hugged him before getting into the driver's seat. Reese headed back to the office just as the bulk of the cars started pulling into the garage. He saw Stanley waiting for him by the door to his office, and Reese clenched his teeth together and felt his heart race at the intrusion he presented.

Stan looked around curiously when he stepped into Reese's office. Reese tried not to let the man's barely concealed snooping bother him. He knew that he'd be looking everywhere as part of the investigation. Stan handed Reese a paper as he wandered back towards the lockers. Reese glanced at it. He knew what it said: Lester had privately hired Stanley Charles to review and assess the evidence with the car theft. Since there wasn't much evidence apart from the car itself, Reese had to admit he'd be surprised if the whole investigation took more than the afternoon.

It seemed like overkill to Reese. People had their cars broken into all the time. You learned, and you moved on. There was nothing more to it than that.

Stan had rolled up the sleeves of his button-down shirt, revealing a sleeve of ink on his left arm. His height and build proved intimidating enough, but Reese wondered if he had the tattoos to enhance the effect.

"So, I'm supposed to give you free rein of my entire workspace just like that?"

The actual theft aside, he'd always prided himself on maintaining a well-managed work area. He knew it'd be better to be fully cooperative upfront, but it was more the consistent nature of the man whose car he had broken into that made him furious and defensive towards Stanley. Hadn't Reese proven himself that morning by helping those two women? He took pride in his garage, in helping people, even if most weren't as thankful as the women this morning.

Stan shrugged. "Just doing my job, but I gotta say it seems like a pretty easy case. It shouldn't take me more than a couple of days to finish everything up." Stanley walked back towards where Reese stood near his desk and leaned his hip against a filing cabinet. "I was hoping to look at the security footage of the night. I'll try not to get in your hair, but I would like to walk around the garage with you to see if I can spot anything that you might have missed."

Reese sat down and made himself more comfortable. "Right now?"

Stan shook his head; his lips pulled downward in a frown. "Nah, I have some stuff to finish up today. I just wanted to come in and introduce myself."

Reese nodded and swiveled around to the drawer where he kept the tapes of security footage. "You got a VCR player?"

"Might have one in my basement." Reese handed the tape to Stanley, who took it before holding his hand out to shake.

"Nice to meet you, Reese. I'll take a look at these and get in touch with you tomorrow about a tour of the garage." He turned to go but paused as he came to the door. Reese was about to ask him if something was the matter, but Stan tapped the name of Reese's boss on the certificate by the light switch. "Short guy, right? Balding. Always looks like he's about to start crying?"

Reese nodded, surprised at the accuracy of the description, even if Reese hadn't seen the man in several years. "Spot on, actually." Reese walked closer and stood next to Stan, looking up at him. "Do you know him?"

Stan nodded, a puzzled enjoyment flickering around his mouth. "He's my next-door neighbor." Stan shook his head and glanced over to Reese before nodding. "Have a nice day, Reese."

"You, too, Stan."

Reese saw nothing more of Stan for several days, and he couldn't help but wonder if Stan would be as troublesome as he first anticipated. Reese had expected the man to return almost immediately. Reese didn't return to the bar. His confrontation with the woman still made him clammy when he thought about it. He wanted to go back for Millie Rae. To see her smile at him in that friendly way, but Reese just didn't see how he could manage it. He had no idea how Naomi was watching him, but he had no doubt the bartender would be keeping tabs on him if he showed up again.

He wished his first meeting with Millie Rae hadn't ended so sourly. His departure had made him feel forgotten, as if he were slinking away from an encounter that he hadn't been entirely welcome to in the first place. He could still see the light of the

Rouge Palace through the window of his bedroom. He could hear the bass thumping music, and he tried to picture Millie Rae dancing to that beat. The more he tried to imagine her as her persona of Lady Rouge, the more difficulty he had holding her in his mind's eye. Lady Rouge blended in with the lights and music. She belonged there, but Millie Rae stood out from the decor, smell, and bar. She seemed clean. Maybe it was her preference not to wear makeup when she was off stage, but Reese could only see her as Millie Rae. Even though he had initially seen her as Lady Rouge and had been attracted to her because of her performance, he had to admit that getting to know her as Millie Rae later that night had a more profound impression on him.

It was ultimately her kindness, Reese reflected, standing at his bedroom window, teacup in hand as he watched the dancing lady above the sign. Most of the women in his life had found his more feminine appearance to be troubling. Maybe it was because they couldn't tell if Reese's physical ambiguity meant that he was also fluid on the sexual scale as well. Nonetheless, Millie Rae had simply looked at him. Not his thin nose or hollowed cheeks.

Reese was waving to the two cleaning ladies as they made their way towards the building when he noticed Stan's silver truck sitting in the hatched yellow spot he'd parked in several days earlier. Reese glanced around, looking for the tall man, but he was nowhere to be seen. Frowning, Reese hurried to his office, hand reaching into his pocket for his keys when a hand on his shoulder made him jump.

"Hey, Reese. How's the morning treating you?" Stan's level voice calmed Reese down slightly as he turned to look at the other man.

Reese had to smile at him. Stan had a likable quality that was hard to resist. Still, Reese took a step back and shrugged. "I noticed your truck when I came in. Where were you?"

Stan waved his hand in a vague gesture that encompassed the garage. "Just taking a look around." Stan followed Reese as he turned and headed towards his office. "You jumped like a rabbit. Something bothering you?"

Reese turned into the office, using the moment to gather his thoughts, and motioned for Stan to join him inside. Reese hadn't been particularly bothered that morning, a rarity since the run-in with Naomi, but now that Stan had questioned him, Reese couldn't help but glance out towards the direction of Rouge Palace. The threat of Naomi's watchful gaze had gone from a high whine in his brain to a mild buzzing as nothing seemed to have changed in his day-to-day activities, but Stan's questioning brought it forward with a prick of sweat and a racing heart.

"Nothing much. Just takes me a while to wake up in the mornings."

Stan nodded, seeming not to notice Reese's tone, and grabbed a metal fold-up chair and sat down. He pulled out a cigarette and stuck it in his mouth. Reese raised his eyebrows when Stan didn't bother to light it. Stan shrugged and folded his arms.

"I quit after my divorce. Kind of. But I don't like starting a business meeting smelling like smoke, so it's mostly habit."

"Business meeting?"

Stan's eyebrows rose, and his cigarette dipped as he frowned. "Mr. Lester didn't say anything to you about this?"

"He might have mentioned it," Reese lied.

Stan nodded and glanced behind him as several other employees passed by, laughing loudly.

"He said you'd have the papers I need with the items'

descriptions."

Reese almost sighed out loud and nodded, turning to his desk to get the paper Stan wanted.

"I get the guy's pissed his car got broken into, but don't you think he's a bit pushy?" Stan asked.

Reese glanced over his shoulder at Stan and got the feeling that Stan genuinely wanted to know his thoughts. Reese thought about ignoring the question, the conspiratorial slant of the question seemed petty, but he reveled in being part of the group that mocked rather than the one that got mocked, so he answered.

"A bit."

The silence that followed made both men shift awkwardly in their chairs as they waited for Lester to show. "Ah, I talked to Bill about you." Reese turned and handed Stan the paper. "Thanks."

"How is he?" Reese reached over and picked up his tea thermos, blowing on it before taking a sip.

"He's good. Said to say hi." Stan rubbed his eyelid as he looked over the list Reese had handed him. "Said he was a little sorry you were still here. Thought you were too nice to the people in this place. Wanted to know if you had a girlfriend."

Reese chuckled a little bit at that. "He was always giving me tips to help me date."

Stan handed back the paper. "How'd that work out for you?"

Reese raised his eyebrows. "I didn't say the tips were any good."

Stan laughed, and the sound came out loud and deep, bounding off the walls of Reese's tiny office. Stan shook his head, "I can't imagine they were. Tell you what, we'll grab a beer some night. I'm sure I can offer a few pointers."

Reese let the offer sit with him for a few moments. He hadn't been invited out for a long time, at least not with someone else doing the asking, and it felt nice to be wanted. "Sounds like a plan."

When he did show several minutes later, he was breathing heavily and leaned against the door jamb for a few moments. He was so taupe and boring that Reese couldn't help but wonder if he wore an identical suit every day.

"Can I sit?" He put his hand on the back of Stan's chair, almost pushing the other man out of the chair with his request alone. Stan blinked, and Reese felt almost victorious that Lester was as rude to Stan as he'd been to him. Stan stood up awkwardly, and Lester sat. The chair squeaked, and the legs ground against the cement flooring under the increase in weight. "You've looked at the tapes. What did you find?"

Reese watched the muscles in Stan's jaw twitch. Stan coughed and straightened his shirt.

"Now," Stan began, "the tapes showed nothing. The cameras are designed to face the entry and exit of the garage, at the elevators, and the doorways leading from the stairs. Ideally, you should try to park your car on a higher floor, under one of the fluorescent lights, and not leave valuables inside."

"I know that," Lester interrupted sharply. "I was running late that day and forgot to grab the stuff. So, sue me. Everyone leaves stuff in their car on occasion."

Stan pursed his lips. "Regardless, you hired me because your car was broken into, and your stuff was taken. I'm just telling you safe practices you can use from now on. Because the tapes showed us nothing of value, I'm not sure what other assistance I can offer on that front. Your list of valuables, on the other hand." He waved the paper. "I might be able to do something about that. Your GPS is a high-end model, and since I'm assuming the person who broke into your car was looking to make some quick cash, I can check around the local pawn shops and let the owners know to keep an eye out for it."

Lester leaned forward, and Reese saw him change from an obese, blustering man to a predator spotting unsuspecting prey. "We could catch the guy in the act. Find this sonofabitch and arrest him. I want him charged."

Stan quickly held up a hand. "In an ideal world, yes. But I've been doing this a long time, and I know the guys who do grabs like this. I already stopped by their places."

"You're aiding criminals?"

"You hired me, remember?" Stan snapped. "I will still look for your things, but I won't be insulted. I did look into the liability the garage or your company had in reimbursing you for the items stolen, and it seems as if the garage claims no responsibility. You might be able to negotiate with your business. That'll have to be between you and them. I'll snail mail you my contract to sign, and I'll send you a copy in your email. Please sign it after you've read it over. Do you have any questions?"

Lester quietly stood, not bothering to shake Stan's hand, and left.

Both Reese and Stan stood there in silence for a few moments.

Stan drew Reese's attention back to the present when he sat in the seat Lester had recently abandoned. "Christ, I thought he was going to punch me. People like that don't like hearing that they've been had. I do think the office workers could do with a crash course on general vehicle theft prevention." Stan sat down, muttering more to himself than to Reese. "Maybe the company would be willing to let me do an hour-long crash course. I saw several cars with items in plain view." He frowned and shifted in his seat. He grimaced, returning to his surroundings, and glanced at Reese with a disgruntled look on his face. "I always get kinda grossed out sitting on a seat someone else just left. The warmth makes my germaphobe brain think I'm sitting in someone else's farts."

Lester persisted, dropping by randomly asking for any updates. His window had been fixed the same week of the break-in, and Reese took little pleasure in telling the man that nothing had changed. He almost wanted to lie and say that the culprit had been found to get the man to leave him alone. Reese knew that Lester was pestering Stan almost as much, but Reese preferred zero contact with the overbearing man.

Reese was walking back from taking out the trash when he saw Stan waiting by his office. It was past seven, so Reese frowned and picked up the pace. The weather had taken a turn, and the light jacket that Reese had on did nothing for the brisk wind that came through the gaps in the concrete. He saw that Stan was wearing a heavy, work-worn denim jacket over his pressed white shirt. He turned and saw Reese approaching, raising a hand in greeting before digging in his pocket and pulling out a pack of cigarettes. Reese saw the red of the flame and the rise of smoke as he came within speaking distance.

"Is everything all right?" Stan looked relaxed enough, but the out-of-place appearance had concerned him.

Stan nodded as he took a pull on his cigarette. "Yeah. Why? Just thought I'd stop by and see if you wanted to grab that drink I mentioned."

Reese stood there, still holding his broom and dustpan. "I figured you had only said that in passing." He stepped past Stan to his office, his face feeling warm because he knew the comment had meant to sting a little.

Stan followed him inside the office, catching the door with his hand before it swung shut. "C'mon, Reese. I'm not an asshole. I said I wanted to grab a drink with you. You have a date or something tonight?"

Reese finished setting his stuff down and turned to Stan. "I just haven't hung out with anyone in a while."

"Well, poor you." Stan joked, tossing the end of the cigarette in the trashcan. "Look, you're a shut in. I get it, but you aren't helping yourself just going from work to home and back." Stan tapped an invisible watch on his wrist. "You're wasting valuable drinking time. You won't even have to go far. Let's just go to the bar across the street. Have you been there?"

Reese shuffled his feet and grabbed his jacket. He hadn't been back since that night in the alley. He hadn't intended to go back despite his desire to see Millie Rae, but he couldn't explain that all to Stan.

"One drink," he said, ushering Stan out of the office before locking up. He didn't want to be there any longer than he had to.

"You been to this place?" Stan asked as they quickly crossed the street.

Reese reached for the handle, almost grateful that Stan was with him this time because it might help him relax and get through the evening. "Once or twice. I didn't stay very long," he lied.

He opened the door for Stan and let him go first. Reese glanced behind him towards the alleyway, fully expecting to see Naomi waiting for him. He shuddered and quickly went inside.

There weren't very many people inside. Reese glanced to Stan, who pointed to several seats by the bar. They made their way over and sat down. The bartender was the same man who had threatened Reese almost two weeks ago, and he felt his confidence at returning vanish. Reese glanced over to Stan to see what he was doing, but the other man was looking around, his eyes drifting to the dancers on stage and then to the private rooms upstairs.

"You want anything, buddy?" The bartender asked behind Reese's back.

Reese turned, unsure of how the man would treat him after their last encounter, but his face seemed calculatingly neutral. Either the bartender believed his threat to be enough to scare Reese into behaving, or his time away from the bar had been enough to make the woman lose interest in him. Reese wanted to tap Stan on the shoulder and tell him they should go somewhere else. Anywhere else. He glanced at Stan, who was watching the dancers again. Reese's shoulders slumped in defeat, and he turned back to the bartender.

"Just two dark beers, please."

Reese watched the bartender a little longer as he filled the glasses and brought them back. The man seemed wholly nonplussed that Reese was sitting at the bar. Reese had been on edge since the threat, but maybe that was all it took to keep people like him in line. When you were someone who jumped at your own shadow and had little social interaction, maybe the threat of surveillance was all that was needed. Reese hadn't seen anyone lingering around the garage or his apartment, so with any luck, they'd concluded he was a no one and decided to leave him to his own devices.

Reese thanked the bartender, who nodded, tossing two coasters their way before continuing down the bar to help someone else. Feeling momentarily protected by his nonthreatening nature, Reese grabbed Stan's beer and got his attention before handing it to him. Stan glanced down and took the beer, taking several deep gulps before setting it back on the bar. The drink had drawn Stan's attention back to Reese, and he turned away from the dancers entirely.

"So, how long have you been at the garage, Reese?"

Reese turned in his seat to match Stan and set his drink on the coaster the bartender had provided. "Pretty much my whole working life. Got hired there soon after getting out of high school." He had been nervous about opening up; the shaking in his hands confirmed it. It felt so welcoming to sit here and talk to someone, to have someone wonder about his life. "How long have you been a private investigator?"

"Five years, give or take. I got out of the police force. It just wasn't right for me, but this has been a good setup for me."

Reese nodded and took another drink of beer. "You said at one point you were married?"

Stan chuckled and nodded. "Yeah, thought it was what we wanted. It turns out she thought being married to a cop would be more romantic than what it is. Especially when the cop you're married to does mostly filing and desk work." He took a long drink of his beer and motioned for the bartender to get another one. "It would have ended anyhow. Better it ended sooner rather than later."

"So, are you the guy I would talk to if I had concerns about someone following me?" Reese could see Stan's eyebrows raise at that. Reese felt clammy just asking Stan about Naomi's potential threat, but he needed someone to talk to about his current situation, and Stan felt like the only person he could trust. Stan nodded and took another drink. Reese twisted a napkin in his hands, ready to tell Stan what had happened in the alley, but the bartender interrupted them by clapping a hand on the bar in front of them.

"You boys good?"

Stan nodded, but the bartender kept his eyes trained on Reese, his presence feeling more and more constricting.

"We're fine," Reese said softly. The man moved away, and Stan turned back to him.

"So, are you really in trouble?" Stan's face had smoothed into a focused seriousness that both touched and scared Reese.

Reese chuckled; his throat dry. "Look at me. I'm not the kind of guy who gets into trouble. I was just curious."

Stan hummed in the back of his throat as he looked around the place. "You ever been up to the VIP rooms?"

"No, I've only been here at the bar."

Stan set his beer down and clapped Reese's shoulder with a sigh. "See, that's your problem, Reese. We need to get you out more. You won't ever meet a girl if you don't take some initiative."

Reese took another drink of his beer and glanced sidelong at Stan, who was studying him. "You're full of shit."

Stan burst out laughing, the noise drawing the attention of several guests and the bartender. Reese glanced around, feeling ashamed of drawing that much attention to their conversation, but everyone had almost immediately turned back to their drinks.

"It took you a second to realize I was joking," Stan said, waving the bartender over for two more drinks.

Reese was about to say something, but the lights went red, and he lost interest in anything Stan was going to say. There had been a small kernel of hope that she would be performing tonight, but he didn't want to ask to find out. He swiveled to face the stage. She came on stage in bare feet. It conveyed an innocence that crumbled as he traced his eyes up the rest of her body. The red material made her skin glow. He reached over for his drink and saw that Stan was watching him. Reese opened his mouth to say something but shook his head and went back to watching Millie Rae. Whatever Stan's opinion was could wait until the dance was over, and the dance was over too soon. It felt as though he'd blinked, and suddenly the lights were returning to normal. Reese drank the remainder of his beer as he turned to face the bar.

Stan didn't say anything at first, simply let Reese sit quietly for a few moments before coughing lightly. "She's why you come here?"

Reese nodded. Of all the things Stan could have learned about Reese that night, he felt the most vulnerable about Millie Rae. "I've only talked to her a few times." It wasn't entirely true, but Reese had no idea how much the bartender could hear, so he kept his connection to Millie Rae vague.

Stan glanced back to the stage. "What's her name?"

"Millie Rae."

Stan nodded, turning his glass in his hands for a moment before reaching over and toasting Reese's glass. "To Millie Rae, then. She's got you looking at the world through rose-colored glasses."

Chapter Four

Reese nodded. "Be right back." He left Stan at the bar and went to the restroom.

The restroom was covered in a yellow subway tile that left Reese slightly nauseated when he'd washed his hands and exited. Along the hallway, he stopped briefly to admire the pictures that were tacked haphazardly along the wall. The sentimental nature of the act surprised him, but he glanced at several shots of girls in various styles of costumes marking different decades. Returning to the bar, he frowned when he noticed the bar was empty except for the bartender pulling glasses out from behind the counter. Reese stepped up to the bar and glanced around again, wondering if Stan had gone out back for a smoke.

"Your friend paid and left," the bartender said behind him. Reese turned and looked at the man who was currently running a cloth along the outside of the glasses he'd pulled from the shelf.

"He just left?"

The bartender nodded and turned away, but he paused and turned back. "He also paid for a private room for you and a girl of your choice. Twenty minutes. Let me know who to get when I get back." He turned and walked away, carrying the rack of glasses with him to the other side of the bar.

Reese sat down at the bar and frowned at his folded hands. Disjointed, he glanced around again, hoping that perhaps Stan was playing a joke on him and would appear to laugh at the expression on Reese's face. Stan hadn't even bothered to wait to say goodbye. From what little of Reese knew of Stan, it seemed out of character, but maybe something had come up. Beyond that, he'd paid for Reese to have a private room. That thought seemed to finally sink into his mind, causing his body to break out into a cold sweat. Reese turned and looked up at the dimly lit upper floor of the bar. What exactly was Reese supposed to do? He began folding and unfolding a napkin on the bar as he waited for the bartender to return.

"Who you want me to ask for?" The man drummed his fingers on the bar as he waited in front of Reese.

"Uh, I need a few more minutes," Reese answered, wondering if there were any way he could refuse the offer without feeling guilty about wasting Stan's money. Reese's mounting anxiety turned into an angry irritation that lashed down his spine. Stan should have even asked if that was something Reese wanted. Reese crumpled up a napkin in his hand and ground his teeth as the bartender continued to move around.

"Millie Rae," Reese said to the man as he walked by with a drink order. As much as he wanted to avoid Naomi finding out any more about their time spent together, he couldn't just let his disappearance go without an explanation.

The man nodded. "I'll call backstage when I get back from dropping this off."

Reese swallowed, not entirely sure that he made the right decision. Reese watched from his seat as the bartender lifted a phone from the counter and spoke a few words into the receiver before putting it back down. The man reached up and pulled a key down from a row along the wall. He sat in front of Reese.

"Go on up—room three. There's a menu up there about any extra pricing. She'll be upstairs in a few minutes."

Even though he'd been given the all-clear to go upstairs,

Reese felt locked to his chair. His mind swirled with the thoughts of what Millie Rae might or might not know about Naomi and whether even to bring it up. Best just to say goodbye and let Millie Rae be none the wiser.

In the end, he tightened his hand around the key and walked up the stairs before he could find an excuse to leave. The key jammed in the lock, and when he pushed inside, the room was dark, the air humid, and he desperately wished for a fan overhead. Still, he sat himself down on the cheap love seat. The walls were whitewashed, and the carpet held on to the smell of cigarette smoke with aged determination. He rubbed his hands along his thighs and stood, not liking how his shirt bunched around his stomach while sitting. He was reaching down to look at what the extra menu entailed when he heard the door open. He swung around, the paper falling from his hand as he watched Millie Rae walk in.

She had changed out of the costume he'd always seen her wear on stage. Instead, she wore a sheer black robe that concealed only where the fabric folded in on itself. The bra and tight shorts she had underneath were also black, but something in the material glittered. Her hair was loose, natural, and beautifully full around her shoulders. Now that he saw all of her up close, he could see things he hadn't been able to on their previous talks. She had a small birthmark on the inside of her left hip, a web of stretch marks trailing up her side, but when he focused on her face, Reese saw that her eyes were that same clear gray that he'd seen before. Dove gray. Her nose was bent, and Reese wondered if she'd broken it as a child. Her mouth was full, painted light pink, and it took him a moment to realize that she was speaking to him.

"I'm sorry," he said, dropping his gaze back to his hands. "I didn't hear what you said." The couch dipped as she sat down and patted the seat next to her, encouraging him with a small smile to sit down next to her. He did, and his face warmed with how close she was. He looked sideways at her, staring perhaps a bit too long, trying to drink her in as a tired bird might drink in a stream on a hot day.

"I said that I was surprised to see you here." She ran a hand over her hair. "You just suddenly stopped showing up, and I thought maybe you'd lost interest." She dropped her hand and moved closer. "Gotta say, though. I didn't expect you to have you request me up here." Her voice was softer in here, perhaps the room lent itself to quiet talk, or maybe she didn't have to shout to be heard over the music downstairs.

"Ah, well." Reese trailed off, not quite sure where to start. "A friend bought me the room," Reese said, his eyes tracing the way the black robe curled around her neck.

Millie Rae laughed. "Well, Reese, I can't decide whether I'm insulted or flattered." She leaned back into the arm of the couch and stared at him. "Why did you stop showing up downstairs?"

Reese stood, feeling like his body was attached to an electric outlet.

"I didn't mean to make a mess of things. And I didn't mean to stop showing up, but I think I messed up."

"Why don't you tell me what's going on."

It took Reese several attempts to get the full story out, but when he finally did, he felt exhausted. He sat down on the couch next to Millie Rae and put his head in his hands.

"I didn't want to tell you, but doing that seemed more stupid."

"Well, you're right that ever since Naomi took this place over, it's been rough. She lets her crew do whatever they want with us. We don't mess with the dealing, but Naomi sure tries to get the girls hooked on the stuff so that she has an easier time controlling them."

"I tried to convince her that we weren't close, but I'm not sure that she believed me. I don't know what to do. I will stay away so that hopefully she'll forget about me, and you'll be able to stay clear of her, but I don't even know what to expect."

Millie Rae glanced at him and smiled. "You know, Reese. You're a good man. But yes, stay away. I'll be safer that way, and hopefully, Naomi will find other things to occupy her time."

She reached out and took his hand. They stayed that way until her time was up.

Reese fought hard to resume his regular schedule. The threat from the landlord about eviction was still looming over him, and even though the man hadn't demanded payment, he would watch Reese coming and going from the apartment with narrowed eyes. As it stood, he had five dollars for the next ten days. His pantry was running low on instant noodles and saltine crackers. He'd applied to several mechanic positions, knowing his way decently around a car, but he hadn't heard back, and there wasn't the luxury of being picky. You took what paid the bills. Since his disappearance from Rouge Palace, he hadn't spoken to Stan, but Reese hoped that he would stop by again.

Reese was busy cleaning up his desk in front of the security cameras when he heard a knock at the door. He turned, knowing it wouldn't be Lester because he never was kind enough to knock. Reese recognized the man standing in the doorway. He had constantly reminded Reese of a French Bulldog with how his short, husky stature radiated an air of gruffness, but it disappeared when he smiled. His whole face opened up, and he had one of the loudest laughs that Reese had ever heard. He was a board member of the business connected to the garage. Reese had seen him come and go every day, and his parking space was positioned as close as possible to the door. He would occasionally wave to Reese in the mornings, but Reese always knew when the man was in the garage because his laugh bounced up through the levels and out the front gate.

"I hope you don't mind me stopping in."

"Ah, no. Would you like a seat? I'm afraid all I have is that fold-up chair."

At that moment, Reese saw what his shabby office must look like to someone who took their lunches in a boardroom. He tried to dust regularly, but the office nonetheless seemed consistently unclean. Even Reese's offer of a chair felt humiliating. The man's slacks probably cost more than three months of Reese's income, and Reese honestly couldn't imagine the man taking a seat in the chair that leaned against the wall.

The man shook his head and took a step farther into the room. Sweat beaded up on Reese's forehead as the man came into the room. Reese resisted the urge to back up and allow the man more room. It wasn't that he was intimidating. It was his position, so far above Reese's, that had his hands go clammy.

The man gave him a smile that quickly reached his eyes, and he pulled an envelope out of his pocket before handing it to Reese. Reese took it tentatively and thanked the man. He checked the time on the clock above Reese's computer and sighed.

"I'm afraid I don't have time to hang around, but I wanted to give you this. You've been such a help working with that man that Lester hired, and you've done far more than what this job has asked of you. It's come to light that some of our staff appreciate what you do, helping them with their cars and all that. There's an offer in there for you that we hope you won't refuse."

Reese took the envelope. He immediately noted how heavy it was and how nice the paper felt in his hands. Whatever was in the envelope, they had taken the time to use heavyweight paper. Reese felt his armpits tingle with sweat. He didn't care to open the letter while the man was watching. Instead, he set it on the desk next to him and shook the man's hand. The man turned to leave but paused, pointing at the improvised award Stan had noticed the first time he came to the office.

"You're a good man, Reese. Shame it's taken us so long to notice." The man waved behind him as he left and headed towards his car.

Reese let the unopened envelope lay on his desk. He stared at his name written on the front in cursive. He hadn't seen cursive since grade school. Didn't know anyone who used it anymore, but the letters looked confident, like they always wrote cursive. That certainly didn't matter in the long run, but it impressed Reese. Who was the kind of man to write in cursive daily?

He let the anticipation of the unopened letter weigh down his pocket as he closed up for the night and headed home. He kept his hand on the envelope as he walked up the creaking stairs, foolishly afraid it might float away on the light breeze. He was digging in his pocket when he heard the creak of the stairs below him. Turning, he saw the landlord staring up at him, cigarette in his mouth.

"You got that rent money for me yet?" Reese didn't bother with a response; he simply opened his door and stepped inside. "Your time's coming up," the man called before Reese shut the door.

He set the envelope carefully on the table before making himself stick to his usual routine of hanging up his jacket and making some tea before finally sitting down. He set the mug next to the envelope and fiddled with the handle until it was in just the right spot. He straightened his hair and took a breath before reaching out and carefully opening up the flap, afraid to tear the envelope more than necessary.

He loved this feeling — the swell of anticipation before the climax. Like sex right before the orgasm. Reese always thought the expectation better than the finale. Something was going to come from tonight. He looked around at the apartment. It had never really been his. Almost all the furniture had stayed right where his parents had placed it when they'd moved in here. Calculating everything that was in the apartment, seeing how he'd been paying rent to his family's memory all these years, giving himself up in bits and pieces while getting nothing in return, he looked down and pulled the papers out of the envelope and began to read.

Reese's hands tightened on the paper as he read. A raise. He'd gotten a raise. All his hard work, all those fixed tires, and gallons of topped off windshield wiper fluid hadn't been in vain. A thirty percent raise. He got up from his chair and paced to the kitchen and back. He sat down again and picked up the paper, carefully reading through all the text again, just to make sure the offer hadn't changed since the last time he read it. Hands shaking, he set the paper down on the kitchen table and cried. He would no longer have to deal with the threats of his landlord. He'd be able to pay rent without relying on his parent's underhanded deal. He would be an official tenant. He glanced around the apartment again, rubbing his eyes with the palms of his hands. He did some rudimentary math in his head. A thirty percent raise, far overdue now that he was adjusting to the idea, meant he could replace the couch and eventually the T.V. Before that, he'd throw out his twin-sized mattress. He looked back down to the paper, rereading it, savoring the words and numbers on the page. He took the paper and carefully stuck it to the fridge, straightening it so that it was just right before he turned off the lights and went to his bedroom.

Reese woke late the following day, got dressed, and walked down to the gas station on the corner to pick up the newspaper. Returning to his apartment, he hesitated as he passed the landlord's office but shook his head and continued up the stairs. He wanted to savor the upswing in his fortune by himself for a while. Sitting at his kitchen table, he sipped his tea slowly and looked through the paper. The local furniture store was going out of business. He dog eared the page and continued flipping. Nothing exciting stood out to him, but he sat and finished his tea anyway.

It took two bus changes to get to the furniture store. He had put on a nicer shirt and tucked it in. He'd rehearsed in his mind on the ride over what he would tell the salesperson. No, he wasn't planning on buying today, but he was looking for a small sofa and bed for his new apartment. He would probably stay in his current unit if he could help it, and the landlord had said improvements had to be made, so the facelift would undoubtedly make the place feel new. It was a little white lie, but nothing so important that the salesperson needed to know.

A huge closing sign greeted him as he approached the store. The parking lot was packed with cars, and he saw several people walking out with loads of bags under their arms. He pushed his way into the building and started towards the sofas sitting in a showroom to his right. The salespeople were all busy, so he looked through the choices quietly. He moved towards a pale couch that had a clearance sticker on it. He stepped out of the way of a couple walking past, talking quietly, but not quietly enough that he couldn't hear their conversation.

"This stuff is so cheap. We'd pay triple this price where we live now," the man was saying as he took the woman's hand and pulled her along.

"We need to buy it before someone else does. I want to put it in the second living room. I can't believe we've never come to this part of town."

"Because it's not a good part of town, that's why we haven't, but I heard the store is going out of business because they're redoing this whole shopping center. Tearing it down, putting in something nicer with all the money that's coming into the area."

Reese quickly walked away, pretending to be interested in another couch so that he could avoid standing next to the young couple any longer. He wasn't surprised that the store was closing because something nicer was moving in. With all the new businesses and apartment complexes moving in on the cheap land, the places that had been around for years were being pushed out by rising prices. He gripped a couch and sat down hard, suddenly deflated because the windfall that had just come his way was pennies for the people walking around this place like vultures. Perhaps he was no better, taking the scraps and bits leftover of a business that no longer met the demands of the people moving into the area. He watched people scrambling around the showroom in a new light.

"Can I help you?" a voice asked behind Reese. He turned to see a middle-aged man standing in the aisle behind him.

"Do you know what's moving in here?" Reese asked.

The man shook his head. "Can't say. I know they're going to tear down these old buildings. Thing is, there isn't anything wrong with them. The builder just decided new is better, I guess." The man ran a hand over the lanyard that held his name tag. "You want to look at something?"

Reese shook his head. "I didn't see anything I wanted."

Reese made his way home, more withdrawn than he had been this morning, but he still felt some pride when he pushed his way into his apartment and saw the letter stuck to his fridge. He sat down on the couch, still unhappy with the floral pattern his mother had insisted on but stubbornly unwilling to get rid of it now. He sank back into the well-worn cushions, content, for right now, with being able to sit there without worry.

Walking home several nights later, it took Reese several moments to realize that a group of men were waving to him from underneath the glow of Neon Girlfriend's sign. He felt his spine go rigid, thinking they were somehow connected with Naomi, but as they called his name, he recognized them as men who worked in the building above the garage. Relaxing, he crossed the street, hands stuffed into his pockets.

"You're Reese, right?" one man said as Reese drew up to the group.

The man was slender in the shoulder but had a warm demeanor that made Reese feel instantly comfortable. Reese nodded.

"I thought so. I see you every time I pull in, but I've never really gotten to talk to you. That's Amy and Michael, and I'm Jim," the man said, gesturing to the two other people.

"What are you guys up to tonight?" Reese asked, surprised that his voice came out steady. His nerves of being even this close to the bar had his palms sweating in his pockets.

"Heading to the bar. Cheap drinks, and you can't beat that it's within walking distance from work."

"We're gonna head in," Michael said. He had opened the top button of his work shirt and rolled up the sleeves.

"I'll be in in a second," Jim said as the other two nodded to Reese before heading to the front doors. "You want to join us?"

Reese watched as Michael opened the door for Amy, and they disappeared inside. As much as Reese did want to join them, he knew he'd be risking Millie Rae by showing his face more. Reese shrugged his shoulders.

"Can't tonight." Reese was content to leave it at that, but he felt his mouth opening again and the words coming out before he could pull them back. "But maybe we could grab drinks another day?"

"Yeah, sure. Sounds good. We know where to find you," Michael joked. He turned his head towards the bar. "I'm gonna head in."

"Good to meet you," Reese said as Michael nodded and headed towards the bar.

Reese stood there for a few moments after Michael had entered. The flashing lights of the dancer above him did nothing to soothe him as it once had. He wondered if Millie Rae had done her dance yet. He wondered if she had taken off her makeup and was hanging out in the back with the other girls or if she'd finished for the night and gone home. He tried to imagine what type of home she might have. He couldn't imagine her in a run-down place like his. Maybe her apartment was old, but he could imagine she let the light filter in. She probably slept in in the mornings since her nights were so long. Maybe she even had a plant that she struggled to keep alive.

The sound of people coming down the sidewalk pulled him from his thoughts. He nodded to them as he passed and went to the bar. He turned towards home, taking one last glance behind him before he did so, making a promise to himself that he wouldn't forget to ask Jim and his friends out for drinks at another bar sometime soon.

He heard a click of heels behind him and thought nothing of it until the woman's voice put a halt to his steps as readily as if he'd been encased in ice.

"I think we need to have a little chat about you visiting my bar, Reese."

Chapter Five

Reese stood frozen as Naomi approached him. Her angular face was made more ferocious by the shadows cast from the bar sign. She wore a business suit of charcoal gray, a cream blouse, and carried a small purse on her right shoulder. Reese pressed his lips together and chanced a glance over to the door of the bar.

"We're just having a friendly chat," Naomi said. She had reached him and tapped his cheek until he forced himself to face her. "No need to be so skittish. Besides, I'm going to make you an offer I think you'll find very lucrative." She turned and waved a hand for him to follow. Reese took a step back, his mind already taking him around the corner in the opposite direction of his apartment. "Reese." Naomi's voice pulled his attention back to her. She stood, waiting patiently as if she could see the thoughts that had just been invading his mind. "I found you once. I can easily find you again, and if I have to hunt you down, I might not be as nice as I am right now."

She led him towards a black sedan parked across the street from the bar. She opened the passenger side door. He folded himself inside. The interior was dark, soft, supple leather that still smelled new. He kept his eyes on her as she walked around the front of the car and got in the driver's seat. She took her bag off her shoulder and set it on the backseat. The engine rumbled to a start. They pulled out onto the street, heading for the freeway.

"What do you want with me? I haven't said anything to anyone about that night," Reese lied, thinking of his confession to Millie Rae and his slip up with Stan. "Please, just leave me alone."

She didn't bother flicking on her turn signal as she jerked them into the stream of traffic heading to the east side of town. "I wasn't lying when I said I'd be keeping tabs on you. I had considered just letting you go." She glanced over to him and smiled. "The knowledge that you'd spend the rest of your life looking over your shoulder and judging every twitch of finger gave me a certain amount of joy, but I realized something about you that you might not even realize about yourself. Honestly, it might be your only redeemable quality." She merged over into the left lane. Reese checked the speedometer and saw she was at least fifteen miles over the speed limit. "People seem to trust you. Even the person I have watching you noticed it. Maybe it's because you're quiet that people assume anything they say to you will be locked tight behind that thin line you call a mouth." A car honked as Naomi jerked the wheel and flung them across several lanes of traffic to slide onto the exit ramp. "Maybe it's because you're so insignificant, but regardless, I have a job for you."

Reese stayed silent. He simply looked out the window, wondering if she would slow down enough that he could try and jump out.

"I don't need the silent treatment. You're going to help me. It's a harmless task on this side of town, and here's what I'll give you in return. I won't keep tabs on you. Well, not in the way I have been. If I want to know what you're up to, I'll merely visit you at Rouge Palace or even your work."

Reese jerked his head around and stared at her. It wasn't that he was surprised she knew where he worked. The proximity of Rouge Palace to the garage made separating the two parts of his life near impossible. No, it was the utter calmness in which she'd stated it, not bothering to look at him to see his reaction, as if she already knew what it would be. Her belief that she would be able to walk into the garage and pass herself off without suspicion bothered him greatly.

"And if the threats aren't enough, then I'm sure we can come to an agreement where Millie Rae only offers you her special services. I do know how attached you are to her. Knowing the whore you're so enamored with could be sucking off a guy right before she visits you would undoubtedly leave a sour taste in your mouth." The side of her mouth ticked up in a smile. She rolled through a stop sign and turned left into a group of older neighborhoods. "Or I could promise to punish her for your unwillingness to help you. It's ultimately your choice on how amenable our relationship plays out."

Reese watched the play of light on her face for a moment before speaking. "What do you want me to do?"

Naomi smiled at him, a gash across her mouth, her small teeth shining in the streetlights. "I have a competitor that I need dealing with. You don't need to know more than that, and you won't have to do anything tonight. I'm just giving you a tour of the area so that when I finally do need you, you'll have an idea of where to go."

They drove further down the road, the houses getting larger, older, and markedly more rundown. On one side of the road, opposite the houses, a grove of trees had grown up next to the street. In a break through the trees, he could see that the ground sloped down, and an irrigation canal ran alongside the road.

"My competitor runs his business out of that house," Naomi said, pulling his attention back to her. She nodded to a house out of his side of the car. It stood on the hill, much like the others, but this one was dark, where some of the others had signs of life inside. The yard looked as though it had once held a large garden, but now only weeds and overgrown grass were visible from the glow of the car's headlights. The sides of the house were a light color, and he could see that the front door sported an ornate door surrounded on both sides by faux columns. "It's mostly drugs. Some guns, but those are harder to hide. Regardless, he's trying to take over my territory."

Reese watched the house slide away as Naomi sped away, turning along another street before slowing again.

"What's his name?"

Naomi shook her head. "Not for you to know right now. Careful, you get too curious about the inner workings and you might just find you like this line of work."

Reese ground his teeth together as he continued to stare out the window. "I doubt that."

"Next week, you'll have another private session with Millie Rae. She'll have information for you. Just follow the instructions and you'll not need to worry about Millie Rae's safety."

"Why not just leave me alone," Reese asked, turning to face her. Rage boiled up his back; he clenched his hands, and he momentarily wondered if he couldn't punch that smug look off her face. "You don't need me to do this. I'd probably make some mistake and ruin your plans. I'm sure you could find some other guy to blackmail into this."

Naomi turned the car back towards the highway and sighed. "You're making this harder on Millie Rea than it needs to be. Remember, you aren't the one getting hurt here. I happen to know that she refuses private audiences with one customer in particular. He likes to choke the girls, ruff them up a bit. If you keep pushing me, I'll give him unlimited access to her." Reese was silent for a few moments, chewing over the damage he could cause to Millie Rae if he didn't play along. Finally, he nodded and slumped back in the passenger seat, looking straight ahead.

"Good," Naomi said. "I knew you'd see reason."

The rest of the car ride was silent, and Reese shifted in his seat as they pulled closer to Rouge Palace, thinking she would let him out, but she kept going, and Reese felt his mouth dry out as she pulled into the parking lot of his apartment complex.

"You look a little pale," Naomi said as she waved to a couple of tenants walking their dog. "Get a good night's sleep. I've heard they're doing construction on this place. It's about time. Might be better to just scrape it down to the ground and start over."

He saw the people walking their dog pause and look at him as he got out of the car. He had little idea what they thought about seeing such a nice car in this dump of a place, but he quickly shuffled past them and into his apartment. He barely made it to the bathroom before he was sick.

He didn't sleep. His dry eyes and tired limbs told him as much as he stood at his bedroom window and watched the lights of Rouge Palace shut off for the night. Vague shapes of patrons and workers whispered away into the night. He stayed where he was, a gargoyle perched on his crumbling tower. After several minutes of no more movement, he went to his dresser and dug through his wallet. Pulling out the business card he wanted, he went to the living room and picked up the phone. The droning of the dial tone helped settle a headache firmly between his eyes. He glanced at the clock on the microwave, hesitating at the early hour. He quickly dialed Stan's work number and waited through the numerous rings until the answering machine clicked on.

"Stan, it's Reese. It's late, and you'll get this in the morning, but I need you to call me as soon as you get this. I need help, and I don't have anyone else to turn to." Afraid to say any more than that, Reese hung up after remembering to leave his phone number. Walking back into his bedroom, he curled up under his covers and fell into a tossing sleep.

The blare of the phone pulled Reese out of his first deep sleep of the night. Thrashing out of his sheets, he hurried to the phone.

"Stan?"

"Christ, Reese. This is the third time I've called you. Why don't you have an answering machine? And where have you been? You call saying it's urgent, and then you don't answer?"

"I'm sorry," Reese said, running a hand over his face to wake himself up. "I finally fell asleep and didn't hear the phone. I'm serious about needing your help. Is there some place we could meet and talk? Someplace safe?"

"Come to my office this afternoon," Stan said. Reese could hear the shuffling of papers, and he swallowed nervously at the thought of being on speakerphone.

"Can anyone else hear us?"

"Only me and the dust bunnies underneath my desk. You sound seriously freaked out. Just take a breath and stay in your apartment. I have some meetings this morning I can't reschedule, but I'll see you later today. My address is on the back of my card." Stan cut the line, and Reese forced himself to hang up the phone instead of crushing it in his hand.

Reese hit the buzzer for Stan's office later that afternoon. He glanced around the street. A woman walked by with shopping bags full of cereal. A man was sitting across the road waiting for the bus stop. None of them looked overly suspicious, but then again, Reese hadn't noticed anyone spying on him this whole time, and Naomi had still known precisely where he lived. He hunched his shoulders and turned back towards the building, pressing the buzzer again with a shaking hand. He heard the door click open and quickly went inside. The steps up to the second floor were carpeted and gave off a smell of cigarette smoke. He ran a hand through his hair and took a breath in through his mouth. Landing on the second floor, he saw Stan's name on a plaque and knocked on the adjacent door. Stan's footsteps thumped on the other side of the door, and Reese's tense shoulders sagged a little when Stan opened the door and waved him inside.

Reese stepped into the small room and realized that Stan was relatively well off with his business. Reese had had suspicions about this after seeing how well maintained and fitted Stan's truck was, but he wasn't entirely sure until he saw Stan's office. The chairs that sat across from the desk were upholstered in soft black leather, the desk was a modern chrome finish, and the accents around the room matched the desk. Despite the age of the building, Stan kept his little corner as professional as everything else he owned. Stan walked to a side table just inside the room and gestured for Reese to pour himself a drink. He hadn't spoken yet, and Reese wasn't sure if he should be the first to speak. His mouth felt clogged with all the words that he needed to say, each clamoring to come out so that they all got stuck on each other.

Reese poured himself a glass of water and came to sit in one of the chairs. Stan sat down across from him a moment later with a cup of coffee. They stared at each other for a few moments before Reese felt a nervous smile uptick at the corner of his mouth.

"Do I just start talking about what I need your help with?"

Stan smiled and pulled out a pad of paper from his desk. "Why don't we cover some groundwork first?" He nodded to Reese, who nodded back. "Does the person you are in trouble with know you've come to see me?"

Reese sighed. "I'm honestly not sure. She said she was having me watched, but I tried to be careful coming here."

"People often use the threat of surveillance as intimidation." Stan crossed his arms and leaned back in his chair. "What gives you the reason to believe she, or anyone else, has been keeping tabs on you?"

"She knows where I live."

Stan nodded, leaned forward, and made a note on the pad of paper. "Do you fear for the safety of yourself or others?" Reese nodded, and Stan's hand stilled at Reese's answer to the last question. He set the pen down and searched Reese's face for a while.

"What did you do that caused this person to take such an interest?"

"I saw her talking to someone in the alleyway of Rouge Palace. She said she was having me followed. She's into drugs. I think distribution. She threatened to hurt Millie Rae if I didn't do what she said."

"And you think she'll carry through with her threats?"

Reese nodded, glancing down at his hands. "I don't have anything else. I know her name, or at least I think I do. She's only told me what she wants me to do."

"Which is?"

"To spy on a guy on the east side of town. She says he's a dealer and that he's been aggressively moving into her turf."

Stan got up and moved across the room. Reese closed his eyes, confident that Stan was simply going to escort him out the door. What information he had was so inconsequential that there wouldn't be anything he could do about it. A glass thumped in front of Reese, and he looked up. A cup of coffee, nearly white with cream. Reese glanced to Stan, feeling his brow furrow.

"You looked like you needed something stronger, and I can't give you whiskey during a business meeting, can I?" Stan searched Reese's face before sighing. "Just take a sip. I doctored it as much as possible. Tea isn't going to do you any good. Now, let's talk about what you can do in the meantime. We don't know enough about her to take what you have to the cops. Even if I pulled some string with a few of my friends, I don't think it would amount to much. She's smart, and she's kept you at a distance to protect herself. I can ask around and see if anyone knows about a Naomi, but it might honestly be better for you to lay low and find out what you can."

Reese nodded, trying to swallow through the lump in his throat. He reached out a shaky and took the coffee, holding onto the cup close to his chest. "Stay relevant, but don't ask questions beyond what is going to keep you alive." He turned on his computer and quickly pulled up his calendar. "I've done enough work in the area that I know several drug dealers are struggling over territory. I can maybe get you some additional information this upcoming week, but meeting regularly with me increases your chances of tipping her off." Stan leaned back in his chair and drummed his fingers along his lower lip. "Don't contact me for a while. It's safe to assume she's following you. You took a chance coming here, but I get why you did. If it comes up, you'll have to lie. Give her a situation that would be believable, but not enough information that she can do her own digging. Is there anything else you're worried about regarding her threats towards you?"

Reese shook his head. His fingers wrapped around the coffee cup. He hadn't taken a sip, but the warmth of the cup still felt comforting.

Stan stood and walked him to the door. Reese was about to leave, but Stan reached out and gently took the coffee cup from his hands. "Can't have you running off with a cup that says 'Private Investigator' on it, now can we?" He smiled at Reese. "Keep your head down. I'll talk to you soon."

Chapter Six

Reese looked at himself in the mirror. He had changed into a pair of khaki pants, a simple, collared short-sleeved shirt, and his usual pair of working boots. He told himself again that what he wore would be of little consequence; still, he thought of Millie Rae, wincing slightly at the memory of their last encounter. He locked up the apartment and headed over to Rouge Palace. No doubt Naomi knew that he'd visited the bar, but he prayed Millie Rae would understand that he'd done his best to stay away.

He ordered a Moscow Mule from the bartender and picked up a leftover upstairs menu that some other patron had discarded. He didn't know if Naomi had made clear to the bartender that arrangement they had come to, and Reese wasn't sure how much it mattered. His choice to visit Millie Rae, to get to know her, had been taken from him. Now they were forced together, and that fact soured in his mouth. The bartender came back around and nodded to Reese's empty glass.

"You finished that one off quick. Want another?" The man wiped his hands on a towel and took the empty glass that Reese handed to him. The bartender looked the same as he always did. His dark shirt absorbed all the neon lights and alcohol spills that surrounded the bar. His muscles were well defined, and Reese swallowed, suddenly remembering how easily he'd held Reese still the night he had met Naomi.

The man returned a few moments later and handed over another Moscow Mule. "This one is on the house. Seems you'll be visiting us more." He nodded to a man down the way to waved to get his attention, but he turned back to Reese and tapped the upstairs menu that lay next to him on the bar. "You want me to get Millie Rae? She already danced, so her time is yours."

Reese shook his head. "I don't want to trouble her just yet, but could I send her a drink? Do you know what she likes?"

The bartender studied him for a moment. "I can send her whatever you like, but you know that it's her job to spend time with you. Troubling her shouldn't be anything you're concerned about."

Reese's mouth tightened. "I'd like to send her a drink."

The bartender shrugged. "Suit yourself." He moved away, stopping at the man who had waved at him earlier to take his order. Reese watched as he handed off a drink to the man and then waved one of the waitresses over and set a dark red wine on the tray before the woman headed to the backstage door.

He turned back to his drink, sipping it slower than he had his first. What if she never came out from backstage? Could she just leave without meeting him? He shifted in his seat and glanced to the backstage door once more, almost convinced that he would see Millie Rae trying to sneak out of the bar without meeting him. He shook his head at that thought and took a deep swallow of his drink. The second Mule had been made stronger than the first, and he'd skipped dinner because he was so focused on meeting Millie Rae. , The alcohol quickly spread its influence to his vision and thoughts. He sighed at his drunkenness like one might sigh at a small child who had made a foolish mistake.

He felt a hand on his shoulder and turned to see Millie Rae. He must have focused so much on his drink that he hadn't heard her walk up, but she had the drink he'd ordered for her in his hand. He smiled a little.

"It seems I have an admirer." He could see the fake bravado in her eyes and at the corner of her mouth. He desperately wanted to rub that sense of unease away with his thumb, but he did nothing. It seemed that she hadn't forgotten about his outburst the last time they'd met, but regardless, she'd have to play her part as Naomi dictated. He hated himself for dragging her into this mess, but he took in her wild hair and suggestive clothing and felt all the worse for the joy of knowing that he had her all to himself.

He moved over, intending to give her his seat, but she waved him off.

"Why don't we just head upstairs? That way we can talk in private." She turned and asked the bartender to top off her drink before turning back to Reese.

Unable to say no, Reese quickly ordered two more drinks before the bartender had a chance to walk away. The walk up the flight of stairs made him feel as though every pair of eyes were on them. He wondered how many of those eyes reported to Naomi.

Closed inside one of the rooms, Reese set his glass down on the table. He eyed the couch, opting to stand as Millie Rae sat, pulling out a piece of paper tucked inside the strap of her bra.

"So much for keeping your distance," she said as she sat down next to him and held the paper out. "But it sounds like you came back for good reasons. At least, when Naomi talked to me, she sounded irritated at how 'chivalrous' you were being. Her words, not mine."

"You don't think of me as chivalrous?"

"No. I live in the real world. I don't need some man coming in to save me. I've done that on my own for long enough. But," she relented, waving the paper under his nose. "I do stand by that you're a good man, and there aren't many of those in this line of work." Reese tried not to think about the fact that he now worked for a drug dealer. Their fingers touched as Reese took the paper from her. He tucked it into his pocket without looking at it.

"Did she say anything else?"

"You can go over anytime next week. Your story is you need to get in the business to pay off gambling debts. Naomi says it should be easy." Millie Rae shrugged. "I don't get a lot of extra info. I'm just the mule in your little game."

Reese saw her shifting her eyes towards the door, no doubt hoping their second round of drinks would come and save her from having a meaningful conversation with him.

"What's your favorite drink?" he asked, far too loudly, startling her.

She glanced down at the wine in her hand. "Gin and tonic, actually, but wine is better to drink since it doesn't mess you up as fast." She took a sip of her drink. "Still, Gin and tonic is my favorite. My grandma used to drink them all the time."

"Do you get to see her very often?" Feeling more comfortable, Reese moved to sit next to her. She moved over slightly, giving him space on the small couch, and shook her head.

"She passed away a few years ago, but she was happy up until then."

"When you said, 'used to,' I just assumed—" he sputtered out. He took a healthy swallow of his drink, simultaneously cursing his sloppy attention to detail and desperately hoping the alcohol would make him forget his fumble.

"Why don't we stick to more normal activities?" she asked, setting down her glass and taking his from him. She turned back to him and moved closer until she was almost sitting on top of him. "That business with Naomi is done." She was slowly unbuttoning the top of his shirt. "And now we have the rest of the time to ourselves."

Reese grabbed at her hands, pushing them away. "I'm not...comfortable with that yet." He sighed and dropped her hands. "I think I was attracted to you at first. But the more we talked, I just liked having a friend. I liked visiting after work. I guess I had this fantasy that we could meet outside of here and get to know each other outside of all this."

"That's a load of bullshit." she snapped, jerking to her feet, blocking his exit. "I believe that you care. And maybe I believe that you think you're doing the right thing, but no client actually wants to get to know us outside of this life." Her voice was bitter, and the line of her mouth soured something in his stomach. "And the real kicker? You don't lose anything in this bargain. Do you know how much money *I'm* losing because of your deal with Naomi? I only get paid when you come around. You may be a good man, but you fail to see the complexity of my situation." She glared at him, her hair seeming to crackle with the energy she was giving off. "So, thank you. I now get to decide between groceries and a mortgage this month without any say in the matter." She reached over and drained her wine. She set the glass down with a hard click before picking up his glass and draining the rest of his drink.

Reese opened his mouth, wanting to defend himself. He sat back down and looked at where Millie Rae stood.

"You're right."

She stared at him for a few moments, eyebrows raised. "I think that's the first time in the history of this establishment that a man realized he was wrong rather than the one being wronged." She raised her hands and clapped sarcastically. Reese said nothing.

They had never had this type of discussion before, and Reese quickly realized that he had still been seeing a mask all those times they'd talked at the bar. Perhaps a truer one than the one she wore as Lady Rouge, but a mask to protect herself from people who only saw what they expected to see. He had thought to protect Millie Rae from Naomi, but it seemed that Naomi had managed to corner Millie Rae in a much more subtle trap than Reese had expected.

They both turned their heads to the door as a waitress knocked and came in, carrying their drinks. Reese thanked her quietly as she set the glasses on the table and removed the empty pair. The girl turned to leave, but Millie Rae got up and followed her, catching the other girl by the arm. Reese watched as Millie Rae fixed the girl's hair and gave her an encouraging smile. Millie Rae said something to the girl in a low voice, and the girl nodded. The door closed once more, and Reese felt the silence hang between them like a challenge.

"I truly do want to help," Reese said, the silence finally driving him to speak.

Millie Rae waved her hand in a dismissive gesture that made Reese feel as if his apology was a gnat batting up a screen door.

"Never mind you helping me. I'll help myself. The way I see it, the sooner I give you the information you need, the sooner I can stop having these meetings with you that continue to cut into my bottom line."

"I feel like every time I try to help you, I end up making things worse for you." Reese ran a hand over his face as Millie Rae returned to the couch and set their drinks down.

"You certainly have done that," she snapped. Her gray eyes were crystal clear as they stared him down. She closed her eyes and sighed. Her body sagged onto the seat next to him.

"Still, if I know anything about Naomi, she's happiest when she has as many people to lord over as possible. This is just giving her a major ego stroking." She ran her fingers over the delicate skin of her inner wrist. "I'll just have to figure out something else on my own."

Millie Rae's fury at being forced to appease his needs made him feel trapped in his skin.

"What did you say to that girl?" Reese asked suddenly.

Millie Rae glanced down at him. "I told her to leave. Naomi wants her to dance, but she's only a serving girl. She won't win against Naomi, and Naomi has very effective ways of keeping her girls in line once she has them." Millie Rae ran her hand up and down her arm absentmindedly before stopping and crossing her arms across her chest. "Still, you better start coming in frequently if I'm to stay on my feet. I've got people to look out for other than myself." She picked up the two full glasses and headed for the door. "Have a nice rest of your evening, Reese, and do remember to tip generously."

Reese took a bus to the east side of town the next week as he'd been instructed. He could feel a line of sweat down his back as he got off the bus and headed towards his destination. Most of the people who got off the bus with him headed towards the businesses. He was the only one who started walking towards the neighborhood. As he passed the lawns, some overgrown, some cut short, he rehearsed his story in his head. He planned on repeating his story over and over until they let him in. He kept the piece of paper with the name he was supposed to use in his pocket but paused and took it out. Standing on the sidewalk, he stared at the name. What if they searched him? Reese imagined the groping hands and the barrage of questions that might accompany someone finding the piece of paper. He shuddered and tore it up, leaving the scattered pieces stuck in a scraggly, overgrown bush near the sidewalk. He just prayed Mitch wouldn't ask too many questions.

The house looked just the same as when Reese and Naomi had driven by the other night. He stood at the foot of the driveway, staring at the house, toying with the idea of simply walking away from it. Away from everything, he knew that if he left, Millie Rae would be the one to blame.

He walked up the sloping drive to the front door. The house must have been well taken care of at some point. There were garden beds that had long been neglected and were full of weeds. There was a pane of glass in the front door, but a piece of yellowed newspaper covered up the cutout. He hit the doorbell twice before realizing it didn't work. Reaching out, he pounded his palm against the door, the wood shuddering in response.

The man who answered the door raised his eyebrows when he saw Reese standing on the stoop. He had on worn jeans and an old shirt advertising a trucking company. His face was tan, with lines that crisscrossed across his face. Almost as if he'd slept wrong, and the sheets had left lines that had forgotten to fade. His lazy eye looked down while the other stared at Reese with unblinking focus. He crossed his arms over his chest and continued to watch Reese in silence. Reese said nothing for several moments before finally taking a breath and plunging ahead.

"I want to talk to Mitch."

The man unfolded his arms and spread his hands wide. It was a gesture meant to convey sympathy, but it merely caused the man to take up even more of the doorway. "Mitch ain't here."

Reese swallowed, shifting his feet where he stood on the stoop. "Let me in, and I'll wait for him."

The man snorted. "You'll leave, and I won't kick your teeth in."

Reese quivered, sweat dripping down and pooling at the juncture of his shirt and belt. "I'll wait right here. Having someone loiter in front of your house won't bring any unwanted attention. I doubt the neighbors will mind."

The man grumbled but didn't move for several breathless moments before he moved to the side and jerked his head for Reese to come inside. Reese stepped into the entranceway, swinging his head from side to side, taking in the tile flooring, the aged paint on the walls, and the smell of grime that seemed to be coming from the carpet in the living room.

The man directed him into the living room before following him in and pointing to one of the several mismatched chairs around the room.

"Sit." The man left after watching Reese take his seat.

Reese sighed and quickly looked around. The room was furnished with chairs, an outdated couch, and a coffee table that sported numerous water rings on its top and seemed to be leaning to one side. The room smelled of cigarettes and stale sweat. He could see the stairs to the second floor from where he sat and heard a rumble of voices from upstairs. There was surprisingly little activity going on around the house. Reese had expected it to be busy with people coming in and out, but the place was so quiet he thought that Mitch and the man who'd opened the door were the only people there.

He jerked to his feet when the man thumped back down the stairs and waved at Reese to follow him back up. As he got up to follow, Reese felt as if he was going to a place that he couldn't come back from, even if it was only up a set of stairs, even if his actions weren't of his choosing. He went farther down the hallway and followed the man into what must have once been a bedroom. The floors were wood, and the blinds in the room pulled closed. A cheap folding table sat in the center of the room, and regardless of what Reese had expected of Mitch, he hadn't expected him to be so organized.

"So, what can I do for you?" The man had to be Mitch. Reese studied him for a moment. Naomi appeared instantaneously dangerous, while the man in front of him seemed hardly threatened by Reese's sudden appearance.

"I want a job with you," Reese said. He waited for Mitch to reply. Both men stared at each other for a few moments before Mitch smiled at him.

"And why do you think I'd be so generous in offering you a job? Do you even know the business I'm in?"

"Drugs and guns."

Mitch shrugged. "A generalization, but yes, those are two things I provide. How did you find out about me?"

Reese took a breath, going over the story he had rehearsed one more time in his head to make sure all the details were correct. "Because Naomi sent me to spy on you."

Reese gave it to them for not pointing a gun at him until this point. Upon entering the house, he had expected to find the men inside armed to the teeth, but only after he'd spoken this last bit did he hear the click behind him and see the glint of a gun as Mitch pulled one out from behind his desk.

"I must have heard you wrong," he said, presumably angling his head to the man behind Reese because he felt a hand fall on his shoulder, holding him in place. "You said you worked for Naomi."

Reese shifted a little, the man's mitten of a hand tightening on his shoulder, crushing the bones and tendons together with a creak. "I wouldn't say work for; she blackmailed me into coming here."

Mitch leaned back in his chair, but his relaxed nature did nothing to alleviate Reese's anxiety. "So what? You thought that by coming here and throwing her under the bus that you'd gain favor with me?" Mitch shook his head and turned his gun side to side. "I could shoot you right now and send your body back to Naomi. What do you think, Adam?"

Reese felt the man behind him shrug. "Could. He's pretty skinny. I bet I could just break his neck. Save yourself the bullet."

Mitch stood and came around the table to stand in front of Reese. In the chair, Reese had been unable to tell how tall Mitch was, but their eyes met level with each other, and Reese tried not to let his gaze waver.

"You could give me whatever information you wanted me to feed to Naomi," Reese said, his nerves harsh and dry in his throat. "If I find out anything about her operation, I could give it to you, provided you promise me something."

Mitch raised his eyebrows and glanced back to the man holding Reese still. "He just got here, and he's already bargaining? Cocky bastard, huh?" The man, Adam, grunted in agreement. "Tell you what," Mitch continued, turning around and returning to his seat behind the desk. "How about we offer you our hospitality until I decide what best to do with you, hm?" The hand tightened on Reese's shoulder, and he tried to bend and twist out of the grip. Mitch opened one of the drawers and put the gun away. "Naomi sure sent a sucker to do her dirty work. Adam, throw him down the hall and make sure he keeps his mouth shut."

Reese yelped as the man gripped him across his chest and heaved him out of the room. "Please, Mitch. You've got to help

90

me." Adam hit Reese across the head, not hard enough to knock him out, but hard enough that Reese saw black and red as Adam dragged him from the room.

He'd regained enough of his senses by the time they'd made it down the hallway that he kept his footing as Adam shoved him into the room. There was nothing in the room, the doors removed from the closet, and the window covered with curtains—ratty curtains, but something that no doubt looked normal enough from the road. Adam followed Reese inside, tucking the gun he held back in the waistband of his jeans before following Reese's slow progression back into the room.

"Please, just let me talk to Mitch again," Reese said, uncomfortably aware of how high pitched his voice had become. "I just caught him by surprise. Let me talk to him in a little bit. I'm sure he'll see how good this deal can be for the both of us."

Adam shook his head and dug in his pocket, pulling out a handful of zip ties. Reese glanced down at them and frantically shook his head. "This isn't happening. I can't be tied up." His back hit the wall of the bedroom. He froze, hands held up defensively in front of him.

"Just shut up and stick your hands out." Adam grabbed his hands, holding Reese's wrists together with one of his hands while he wrapped the tie around and pulled it tight, biting into the flesh of his wrists. Reese stayed silent, his shoulders pulled up to his ears as Adam knelt and tied in ankles together. Adam stood and stuffed the extra ties into his pocket. "Now, keep your mouth shut, and I won't shove a towel in, got it?" Reese nodded, and Adam turned to go.

Reese opened his mouth to beg. Asking that they not forget about him and leave him to rot in this room that held nothing but him and an overpowering scent of cat urine. He held his tongue, fear finally bleeding away into rage as Adam shut him, the lock clicking firmly behind him.

Chapter Seven

Reese banged his head against the wall of the bedroom. He didn't know how long he'd been inside, but long enough that his bladder felt tight and his mouth was dry with thirst. He had no idea what they would do with him, and they hadn't come back in to ask him any follow-up questions. He groaned and rubbed his eyes with his bound hands. Adam hadn't bound his ankles, but he wouldn't try and escape. Even it was just Adam and Mitch out there, they had the advantage of two guns that he knew of and potentially countless more. He cursed his own decision to tell Mitch the truth. As much as he didn't want to, he should have listened to what Naomi said and told Mitch the story he'd been given. He had no idea if the outcome would have been any different, but it was the only thing he could fret about while he sat on the stinking carpet. He struggled to his feet and banged on the door.

"Hey, can I get a drink or go to the bathroom?" He could hear someone shuffling on the other side of the door, but no one answered him. He banged harder with his bound wrists, the discomfort adding to the building anxiety he felt. "Hey, I need to piss. At least let me do that. And what's the point holding me in here if you aren't going to ask me any questions? You—" He cut off as the door swung inward, causing him to stumble back and almost lose his footing.

Adam stood by the open door as Reese righted himself. The man looked thoroughly irritated, a deep line between his eyes accentuated by the dim light as he came into the room.

"I thought I told you to keep your mouth shut," he snapped as he reached Reese and grabbed him by his shirt front.

Reese sucked in his stomach and clenched his mouth, but he stared at the man in the face. "I need to pee, and unless you want this room smelling worse, I think it would be a good idea to let me use the bathroom." Reese nodded down to his hands as Adam let go of the front of his shirt. "I can't exactly do anything with my hands bound."

The man snorted and pulled Reese forward by his shoulder. "I tied your hands together in front of you. You'll figure it out if you have to go as bad as you say."

They walked back down the hallway, passing the office, but it was empty when they passed by. The bathroom was across the hallway from the landing, a tiny room with just a toilet and sink. Adam shoved him inside, following a moment later.

"You're not serious," Reese said, watching as Adam closed them both inside the small space. Adam's overweight bulk took up precious space in the tiny bathroom, and his body odor quickly spread with the lack of ventilation in the room. Adam crossed his arms again and nodded to the toilet. Reese sighed and walked over, contorting himself to reach the button and zipper on his jeans. "Look, I think we all got off on the wrong foot," Reese said as he lifted the seat. "If you let me talk to Mitch one more time, I'm sure we could work something out. I came to you guys with the truth because I think we can both see how nasty Naomi can be. She wanted me to spy on your operation." Reese finished and flushed the toilet. He danced around, struggling to get his button done, but finally succeeded and went to wash his hands. Adam moved out of the way, and Reese turned on the faucet. "In any case, what good is it keeping me tied up here. You either have to work with me or get rid of me, and if you get rid of me,

Naomi will know that her spying didn't work. Who knows what she'll do then." Reese looked around for a towel to dry his hands, but couldn't find one, so he wiped his hands on his jeans. "You might as well try and convince Mitch to give me one more chance—or else we're going to have to do this again at some point—and I'd rather not, if it's all the same to you."

Reese didn't know what Adam said to Mitch, but after he'd returned to his room, Mitch had come by and cut his ties with a box cutter. He gestured for Reese to follow him, and they returned to the office. Mitch was no longer sitting behind the desk. He stood in front of it, hip resting on top as Reese and Adam came in. Reese scanned his face, hoping he might see something there that indicated how this second meeting would go, but his face was unreadable. Adam grabbed his wrists and cut through the zip tie. Blood rushed into Reese's hands, making them tingle. He rubbed them, wincing at the discomfort, but thrilled to be unbound. He put his arms to his sides and waited. Adam stood behind him, same as before, but he was grateful to the man for getting him a second meeting with Mitch.

Mitch stared at Reese, drumming his fingers against the wooden top of the desk for several moments. Reese couldn't decide if Mitch was waiting to see if he would speak or simply deciding what to do with him, but Reese wasn't about to open his mouth until he knew more. Mitch leaned forward, sighing, as he stood up and walked towards Reese. Reese blinked. Mitch was shorter than him by almost a head. For someone who always correlated size with success, it took Reese a moment to adjust. Reese blinked himself back into focus as Mitch waved his hand towards Adam.

"Why don't you go back to the front, Adam? I think we'll be

fine."

Reese felt the air behind him lighten as Adam moved out of the room, closing the door behind him. Mitch walked to the side of the room and pulled out a folding chair. He jerked it open and gestured for Reese to sit. He did, tilting his head up to keep Mitch's gaze in his line of sight. Mitch returned to his position in front of the desk, leaning a hip against it and crossing his arms across his chest.

"What makes you think this meeting is going to go any better than the last one?"

Reese glanced down at his hands. A thin line of red ran around his wrists from the tie.

"I've been tied down since I met Naomi," Reese said softly. He looked back up to Mitch, fully expecting him to laugh at him, but he didn't. Bolstered, Reese took a breath and continued. "She said she was having me watched, and it was true enough because she knows where I live. That's unsettling, but if that had been it, maybe that would have been enough." Reese shrugged, feeling color rise to his cheeks because of what he was going to say next. "But the whole reason I got into this mess was that I met a girl. Say whatever you like, but she's a dancer at Rouge Palace. She seemed to look at me like a person and not like the rat I feel like at work." Reese looked back down at his hands. "Feeling seen isn't something that happens to me all that often, and I appreciated the gesture, even if it is part of her job. I should have been smarter, but Naomi found out. Threatened Millie Rae instead of me. Even if I hadn't felt those things about Millie Rae, I don't think Naomi would have had a hard time convincing me to help her."

"Hurting someone else for her own gain is one of Naomi's greatest skills," Mitch said, startling Reese out of his thoughts.

Reese glanced up and nodded at Mitch.

"Anyhow," Reese continued. "I'd fully intended to do what she asked. I had all the info I needed. She said because people didn't see me she thought I could come in here." Reese shrugged, hoping to loosen the tightness in his shoulders that appeared whenever he thought of Naomi's comments.

Mitch was silent for a few moments before he stood up, walked around the desk, and sat down behind it. "I won't pretend to care about your story. The fact that you fell for a dancer is lesson one of the things you don't do. It can never end well. Still, I have to agree with Naomi." Reese's hands clamped onto his knees, his vision narrowing in on Mitch's face. "I wouldn't have paid you any attention at all. Yet, here you are, and I don't think Naomi could imagine you being anything other than loyal." Reese's hands relaxed slightly. Mitch leaned forward, a flicker of a smile brushing across his face. "You tell her it worked—your little lie. Go back to her. Do what she wants, and you report back to me."

"But what about Millie Rae?" Reese asked, caring little if Mitch thought him weak. "How do I keep her out of this?"

Mitch shrugged, picking at the bed of his nails. "That's your problem. You got yourself into this mess, and the way I see it, the only way to get out is to keep moving forward. Because if you rat on either of us." Mitch leveled a look at Reese. "No one will be able to save you or your whore from being ripped apart."

Reese left the house later that night with an agreement to meet two nights from then and a handshake to seal the promise. Reese stopped at the end of the driveway and glanced back at the house, but the lights were barely visible through the heavy curtains and left him enclosed in the darkness of the night.

Millie Rae was waiting for him in the booth upstairs when he arrived at the bar the next night. She wore the red outfit that labeled her as Lady Rouge, and Reese was glad that he hadn't seen her dance. He sat down next to her, unsure of what was expected of either of them at this meeting. Millie Rae gave him a small smile as if she didn't have the energy for anything more than that for a greeting. Her shoulders slumped, and as Reese took the time to study her face, he saw that her eyes were ringed with red.

"Are you all right?" He put a hand on her shoulder. Her skin was warm, soft, and beautifully dark against his pale hand.

She nodded. "Just a rough night with a girl. One of the perks of my industry is the dancers are often more drugged than their customers." She leaned away from him, not in fear or repulsion, but merely to pull a small notebook from the bag that rested near her feet and placed it on the table. "Naomi wants you to put any information you get in this notebook. I'll carry it to her when you're done, but that's all you're required to do for the night. She doesn't have any other orders for you at the moment." Millie Rae hesitated, her face fixed on the notebook, but she turned and looked at him, and Reese swore he could feel her gaze to the back of his skull. "It worked, didn't it? You got Mitch to take you on?"

Reese swallowed. "I work for him, yes."

Millie Rae sighed, nodded, and handed him the pen. "Good. I wasn't eager about being Naomi's errand girl, but maybe the sooner she gets what she wants, the better." She leaned into the back of the couch and closed her eyes. "Just write down whatever you need to. Wake me up when you're done, hm?"

Reese watched her for a few moments as her breath slowed and her body gradually relaxed into sleep. He always had to be in bed to fall asleep, and he had never been able to sleep next to someone. Even when he was little, he had needed his mother to leave the room after she read to him at night before he could fall asleep. She would finish the chapter, tuck the book just underneath the bed for the next night, and leave, closing the door behind her. Only then had Reese ever been able to relax enough to fall asleep. Now, sitting here watching Millie Rae dose right next to him, Reese marveled at her. Some people could sleep anywhere, but he wondered if it had to do with her earlier comment. He turned to the notebook, tapping the pen on the table for a moment before writing down what Naomi would want to hear. He kept it simple, providing what he hoped was just enough information to keep her satisfied. Finished, he set the pen down, closed the notebook, and leaned back into the couch. A soft snore was coming out of Millie Rae, and Reese smiled as he looked at her. He imagined her like something out of a fantasy, her hair full and flying around her, but it would be an injustice. No, Millie Rae was wholly woman, with the way the swell of her hip beckoned his hand, to the faint whiff of sweat that confirmed she had just finished dancing before coming to meet him, and finally, to the tiny, almost invisible hairs that caught the light around her navel. He reached a hand out and lifted a twirl of hair away from her face, but as soon as he released it, it sprang right back to its original position.

"My grandma always hated that lock of hair," Millie Rae murmured, her eyes still closed. She arched her back, stretching, before opening her eyes and looking at Reese. "She tried everything to get it where she wanted, but short of braids or chopping, it stays right where it wants." She reached up and ran the pads of her fingers along it. "I always kind of liked it, my little rebel lock. It meant I wasn't bound to do the same thing the rest of my family thought I should." She dropped her hand and stood up. "You all done?" She bent and gathered the notebook and pen. "Thanks for letting me sleep. I'll give this over to Naomi." She nodded to him and turned towards the door.

"Wait," Reese said. She turned back to him, one eyebrow raised. "What did your family want you to do?"

She smiled. "My mom and dad wanted me to be a lawyer. I wanted to be a dancer." She turned from him and left the room, leaving Reese in silence to think over this new information.

The old, twenty-four-hour diner had weeds crawling up the sides. Dead grass crunched under Reese's shoes as he walked up the sidewalk towards the entrance. He couldn't see if Adam was inside or not, and he would have liked to wait outside, but the day's heat was flaying his skin and parching his throat. He opened the door; the soft chink of a bell that had lost its ball announced his arrival. A hurried man waved him towards a table near the far corner closest to the kitchen. Reese sat down so that he had a good view of the front when Adam showed. He picked at his nails, trying to think of anything to say to the man. Nothing had happened so far that would interest Mitch or Adam. He nodded to the man who dropped off his water glass before pulling out a menu from the stack shoved behind the salt and pepper shakers along the wall.

He didn't have to wait long before he saw Adam's hulking frame shadow the front door. He moved as he had in the house, a hulking, impressive man based on his size alone, and one who had undoubtedly grown up knowing his size would be his calling card. The few people in the diner glanced at him from over their shoulders and around their coffee mugs. If he noticed, he didn't bother showing it. He kept his gaze on Reese, pinning him to his seat. He sat down across from Reese, the table shifting out of the way of his girth, the bench seats shuddering as they adjusted themselves to the new weight.

He grabbed the water that Reese hadn't touched and drank almost all of it without taking a breath. Setting the glass down, he nodded to Reese in what seemed to be his version of a thank you.

The waiter came and placed another glass of water down. He set a cup of coffee and several plastic cream packets down in front of Adam even though he hadn't ordered it.

"Been here before?" Reese asked as the waiter left. Adam grunted, tearing open three sugar packets and upended them into the mug before tipping in a few drops of cream. He blew on it, the colors stirring themselves together with the force of his breath. He took a sip, nodded, and finally settled his attention fully on Reese.

"How'd it go?"

Reese rubbed the back of his neck, glancing around to make sure no one was close enough to hear them. "Fine, as far as I can tell. Naomi should know that you picked me up by now. I have to write everything I do down for her." Adam grunted, taking another sip of his coffee before gesturing for Reese to continue.

"But that's all the info I have," Reese said.

Adam raised his eyebrows. "Mitch isn't gonna be happy."

Reese ground his teeth together. "What else do you want me to do? I'm sticking my neck out here. You have to give me something to work with if you want me to get any kind of information to you." Realizing he'd leaned forward, Reese sat back and took a breath. "If there isn't anything happening, then what in the hell am I supposed to say?"

Adam shrugged, seemingly unconcerned with the stress that was rising in Reese. "Can't say much to that. I know Mitch is moving product soon, but I tried it, and I know it isn't great stuff. He can't find a good cook. Not like the one Naomi has."

Reese sat silently, watching Adam put more sugar into the cup. "What if I found out the name of Naomi's cook?"

Adam looked up, eyebrows raised. "That'd be good. We had a suspicion of who it was but could never find his location to flip him. You get that," he took a sip of his coffee. "You get that information, and Mitch would probably be very inclined to help you save your girl." Adam finished his cup of coffee and stood. "Get a hold of us when you have the name."

"Wait, aren't you going to pay?"

Adam grinned down at Reese. "This meeting was your treat, according to Mitch." He walked out of the diner, people's gazes following him out.

Reese stayed low and tried not to draw Naomi's attention. As much as he wanted to spend more time with Millie Rae, he avoided Rouge Palace. He came and went from work just like he always had. He ground his teeth together as he made his way up the stairs to his apartment. His landlord had said nothing more to him about eviction, and it was something that Reese wasn't about to bring up. He forced open the door to his apartment and flicked on the light. He was stepping inside when a hand grabbed him front behind and pulled him back out into the hallway.

Of all the people that could have assaulted him at his front door, he certainly wasn't expecting it to be the bartender from Rouge Palace. The man had a frown creased into his forehead so deep Reese wondered how he'd never seen it before. Slammed back against the outer wall of the apartment building, Reese gasped at the pressure on his windpipe. He'd known the man was strong from his last encounter, but there was a fury in his eyes this afternoon that there hadn't been the last time Reese had found himself in this situation.

"You've got a lot of explaining to do to Naomi, assuming I don't kill you first."

He let go of Reese long enough to grab his around the collar and yank him back down the stairs.

Reese hardly had time to gasp air into his abused windpipe before he was thrown into a car and driven the short distance to Rouge Palace. He sat in the car and rubbed his abused throat while watching the other man, trying to figure out just what Naomi knew. The obvious reasoning was that she'd found out about his deal with Mitch, but Reese had a suspicion that when she found out about that, he'd be dead before having a chance to explain himself. Still, he felt his breath begin to hitch in his chest and heavily considered jumping out of the car and trying his fate over at Mitch's.

The neon lights above Rouge Palace were lit in preparation for the evening, but when they entered through the side door, there was no music playing, and the flashing lights that usually accompanied the dancers were turned off. His feet tripped on the carpet as he was drug upstairs and shoved into one of the private rooms. He felt his face grow cold as he saw Millie Rae sitting next to Naomi, looking less than comfortable with her current proximity to her boss.

"Sit your ass down, Reese." Naomi snapped, the sharpness in her voice piercing him through his gut.

He sat across from Naomi and Mellie Rae. His hands clenched on his knees so tightly that he could feel the bones and joints grinding together.

"I didn't do anything."

"You sure as shit didn't. You told Mellie Rae that you'd

convinced Mitch of your story. What I don't understand is why one of my mules is missing from his territory, and you didn't know anything about it."

Reese stared at her, seeing the fury on her face and knowing that if he said anything wrong, Mellie Rae would be the one to suffer for it. "You're deluded if you think that Mitch would have told me anything like that," Reese blurted.

He could see the greedy light flicker in Naomi's eyes. "What did you say?"

Reese stood, shaking with terrified defiance that seemed to come across as his own brand of rage.

"What are you expecting him to do? Confess everything to me as soon as I start? He's not an idiot, Naomi, and because one of your guys goes missing does not immediately make it my fault."

Naomi jerked to her feet, her hands clenched, and Reese quickly positioned himself between her and Millie Rae, who'd been smart enough to move away as soon as Naomi stood. He was so focused on her face that he didn't see her hand swing out until he left the metal of her ring connected with the side of his face. Hot pain lanced just above his eyebrow.

Chapter Eight

Reese held a trembling hand up to his eyebrow and flinched when he saw the red on his fingers. He could feel the tickle of the blood dripping down the top of his eyelid and wiped it away. He glanced at Naomi, who had taken a step back and was rubbing her hand. He took a chance and glanced over to Millie Rae, who remained where she was, but she gestured to her temple, and Reese nodded to tell her he was all right. Naomi turned back to Millie Rae.

"You stay out of this," Naomi snapped.

"So, I'll just go then? Do you need me here?" Millie Rae crossed her arms as she said this, keeping her gaze fixed on Naomi's face.

Reese wasn't all that surprised to see her stand up to Naomi, but he didn't want Millie Rae making the already irate woman angrier.

"Naomi," Reese said, drawing her attention back to him. "I don't know anything about a missing dealer. I can try to find something out, but it might take time."

Naomi turned to him and crossed her arms. "Well, isn't that nice of you. Frankly, I don't have time for you to find out any information. I'm losing money with him disappearing with my shipment, so we're going to set you up in his position until I can find another runner."

Reese stared at her face, her expression unchanging as she stared him down. He spared a glance at Millie Rae and saw that her face had gone ashy in the dim lighting.

"I'll do this on one condition."

Naomi laughed and glanced over to the bartender who'd dragged him in as he rolled his eyes at Reese's statement.

"You're in no position to be bargaining anything at this point in your life," Naomi snapped.

Reese briefly considered lying and telling her that he would give Mitch all her secrets as she had no idea about his current arrangement, but he knew that Naomi's temper was nothing like Mitch's. He'd only met the man once, but Reese had had a sense he could be bargained with. Naomi would go off like a firecracker and blame the victims for getting burned. No, trying to blackmail her in that way would get him nowhere.

"I'll run your drugs for you and continue spying on Mitch's operation if you agree to let Millie Rae visit only me but get pay for a full night's work."

Naomi tapped her fingers along her bottom lip. Reese could see that she was deciding their fates, and he wanted to glance over to Millie Rae to see what her take on the arrangement was, but he didn't dare glance over there and distract Naomi.

"You'd be earning your money back with the deals and gain information from his spying," the bartender said from where he remained by the door.

Reese tried to keep his face neutral. Reese hadn't expected an ally in the man, not after the way he'd assaulted Reese several times now.

"Please don't make me," Millie Rae said suddenly. Naomi raised her eyebrows and turned to her. Millie Rae stepped forward, pleading. "He's awful," Millie Rae continued as Naomi studied her. "He paws at me and has some seriously weird fetishes. I'd rather work a full night in the private room plus dance instead of being required to wait on him to show up whenever he feels like it." Millie Rae turned and glared at Reese, the coldness in her eyes making his own back stiffen in shame.

"Well, if I'm nothing if not accommodating. Reese," Naomi said as she turned her back on Millie Rae. "You'll get what you want. You run the drugs for me, continue to spy on Mitch, and Millie Rae is all yours. I'll make sure she gets full pay. Just to show you how generous I can be. Besides," she said, turning back to Millie Rae, who had hung her head so that her hair partially covered her face, "any chance to remind Miss Lady Rouge that she doesn't own this place is a win for me."

Naomi gathered her things and walked to the door, which the bartender opened for her. Before she left, Naomi turned back to Reese. "I'll give you further instructions within the next day or so. Stay close and wait for me to contact you." She left the room, the bartender shutting the door behind her with a click.

Reese went to the sofa and sank onto it. His small victory over Naomi should have brought him more satisfaction, but with the pain in his face throbbing erratically to the beat of his pulse and the fact that Millie Rae had made it painfully clear how she felt about him, he felt raw and exhausted. He flinched slightly when Millie Rae sat down next to him and gently lifted his face towards hers. She inspected his eye, her brow furrowed. "Bill, you got a clean rag?" She turned as the bartender pulled himself away from the door and walked over, tossing her a rag from his back pocket. She turned back around and gently dabbed at the clotted blood on Reese's face.

"That went about as well as we could have hoped," she said, leaning back to inspect the rag. She leaned forward again and put pressure on the cut, holding Reese's chin in her hand as she did. "It's a good thing she respects your work, Bill, or else she might

106

not have taken Reese's offer."

The man crossed his arms and stared down at the two on the couch. "Like I always say, I gotta watch after my girl." He sighed and ran a hand through his hair. "You good here? I can send up a few drinks, but I should get back down to the bar before we open."

Millie Rae nodded at the bartender. "Thanks for having my back there, Bill."

Bill nodded and quietly left the room.

"I don't know what to think about that guy," Reese muttered as he readjusted the rag. Reese moved away from Millie Rae, taking the rag with him and keeping pressure on his head. "I got it, thanks. I don't need your help."

Millie Rae crossed her arms. "Now, what's this attitude for? This is a win, Reese, and you're skulking like a child."

Reese pushed on the rag, the pain lancing through the emotions trying to somersault out of his mouth. "It's obvious you don't like me. You said as much to Naomi. You didn't get exactly what you wanted, but you don't have to pretend to be happy when she latched you to me."

Millie Rae stared at him for a moment before she started laughing. Reese glared at her, but he couldn't help but feel his mouth quirk up at the sight of her joy. "Well, give me an award. Reese, I knew that Naomi would make you my only option if I said I hated being around you. She hates me. I hate her. But I also happen to be smarter. You're my safest bet, and, coupled with the fact that I'll be making a decent amount every night, this worked out beautifully. I'll just have to remind myself to grumble about you when I'm around the rest of her crew to make it convincing." Millie Rae leaned back and studied him, her mouth still curved upward. "You thought I hated you?"

Reese stared at her from underneath his rag before pulling it away from his face. "Well, now that you say it like that, I feel like an idiot for not seeing it sooner."

Millie Rae patted him on the shoulder.

"You're the kind of kid I would have made fun of in school for being too kind and too gullible. Luckily for you and me, Bill's a decent guy. Sure, he works for Naomi, but he's a softy when it comes to me. Old fart has been here almost as long as I have." She arched her back and stretched. Reese heard her back popping softly.

"What do I do about promising to be her mule?" Reese asked. His feeling of betrayal by Millie Rae out of the way, the threat of having to run drugs for Naomi weighed on him. Just relaying the information Mitch wanted Naomi to know was one thing, but taking part in moving drugs made him want to throw up.

"I don't know, Reese," Millie Rae said. "But I want to help. I truly am grateful for what you did earlier."

Reese nodded. He looked over to her and smiled. "You really did fool me earlier."

She stood and offered him her hand. "There's a reason I'm the main draw for this place. I can fool almost anyone."

Reese thought about calling Stan the next day to tell him what he'd learned; instead, he sat at his kitchen table and drank several cups of tea before calling Mitch. This would undoubtedly be something that he would want to know. The phone rang several times before the line clicked. Adam answered.

"Thought this line was only for emergencies," he said gruffly. "You better be calling with something good."

"I think it is, but I need to talk to Mitch."

"You'll talk to me." Reese could hear the large man

108

shuffling papers on the other side of the line and wondered how much Adam managed for Mitch other than just intimidation.

Reese sighed and played with the bit of string on his teabag. "Naomi knows that one of her dealers has gone missing. She's pissed, and she wants me to take over his position."

Adam grunted into the line, and Reese heard muffled conversation as he spoke to someone in the room.

"Mitch says to come in. Be here as soon as you can." Adam hung up with a click.

Should have just talked to Mitch, he thought as he went to change to leave.

Reese locked up his apartment and headed down the stairs. He saw the landlord coming towards him out of the corner of his eye and gritted his teeth, praying that the man didn't want to talk to him.

"You got a lot of explaining to do," the man said, reaching out and grabbing Reese's sleeve.

Reese felt anger spike through him at the man's touch and jerked his arm away. Reese turned to face the man, crossing his arms and refusing to break eye contact. The man's breath was putrid, smelling of stale coffee and peanuts.

"What do you want? I can pay the new rent pricing. I'll have the updated payments to you soon." Reese prayed that that was all the man wished to talk about, but when he pulled a roll of papers from his back pocket and handed them to Reese with a flourish, Reese knew that his troubles with the man were far from over.

"See, I been seein' you coming and going at odd hours, and some of the other residents got worried. This is your eviction notice on the grounds of you not paying your rent for the past several months. You can leave quick like, or I'll be forced to call the cops."

Reese glanced through the papers the man had given him, feeling like he'd swallowed pounds of rocks.

"This says I have to be out by next Wednesday. That's only three days." Reese crumpled the papers and shoved them back in the hands. "I can't do that."

"You got to. You have no way to prove that you've been paying me at all, and see, I kinda regret letting you slide by with these lowered payments all this time, so I think it's about time to move on. No one wants you here anyhow." The man looked at Reese; the smile playing across his lips meant that he knew full well Reese could do nothing to fight the charges brought up on the paperwork.

"I never liked it here anyhow. I'll be taking my money elsewhere, and I hope you choke on those papers." Reese turned to go, but the man spat on the ground at his feet. Reese briefly considered throttling the man but kept his back straight as he walked towards the bus stop.

Reese banged on the door to Mitch's house, enjoying the way his hand smarted. He shifted from foot to foot as he heard someone coming to the door.

"About damn time," Reese said as Adam opened the door. He pushed himself past the larger man and stomped into the hallway.

Adam shut the door behind him and flipped the numerous locks shut. Reese ignored Adam's raised eyebrows and gestured towards the stairs.

"Do you want to escort me?" he snapped.

Adam shrugged and motioned for Reese to follow him.

Mitch sat in the office just like he had the last time Reese was there. He waved Adam off when they entered the room. Reese crossed his arms and glared at the man while Adam left, shutting the door behind him.

"Why wouldn't you talk to me on the phone earlier?"

Mitch raised his eyebrows and leaned back in his chair.

"Did you have a problem talking to Adam?"

"I wanted to talk to you."

Mitch shrugged. "I was busy." Mitch leaned back in his chair and spent a few moments of silence staring at Reese. "And you're in a fucking mood, which I don't tolerate with grunts like you. You better tell me what the hell Naomi knows about her missing man before I have you thrown out."

Reese gritted his teeth and fought the urge to blurt out his troubles to the man across from him. He wouldn't care, but the news of his eminent homeless weighed heavily on Reese.

"Can I sit down?" Reese asked, gesturing to one of the chairs in front of the desk.

Mitch nodded.

Reese sat, his anger flowing down the chair legs and into the floor. "Naomi knows that one of her dealers is missing. The way she said it, she had the guy running product in your area. She's furious, and she wants me to take over his role until further notice."

Mitch leaned back in his chair and smiled. "Oh, we knew he was running product. I was hoping we'd get him to tell us the name of her cook if we threatened him enough. What did you guys do to him?" Mitch asked Adam. "Break into his car and steal some stuff? Threaten his family?"

Adam nodded as he leaned against the door jam. "Yeah, we ended up just breaking into his car. Didn't bother with the family because it's gotten too messy with all the new badges running around."

Reese turned back to Mitch, who shrugged. "See? We were even civil about it, but when a guy threatens to go to the cops." Mitch shook his head. "You gotta get a little rough. And maybe Adam got a little too rough."

Reese felt his mind rapidly making connections. Had he been so close to this from the beginning and not even realized it? Maybe that's how Naomi had known where he worked. She'd already had people dealing in his vicinity without him knowing. The way they talked about the man reminded Reese of Lester, but there was no way that was possible. The man had been awful, but Reese didn't see him peddling drugs for extra cash on a street corner. No, he realized. It wouldn't have been on the street corner. It would have been inside the business. Deals done inside the bathrooms and in the stairwells of the garage after hours. And who knew where Lester might have dealt inside Mitch's territory. Reese didn't even know how far Mitch's territory went. Naomi held onto her area with a caged fist, but Mitch seemed more laid back, as if he knew that he had no reason to fight for respect from his dealers because his power wasn't under question. Naomi was the underdog between the two, and Reese wondered if he'd been feeling cornered by the wrong person this whole time.

"You seem shook up by the lack of information you got," Reese said, returning to the conversation, his hands clenching into fists on his legs.

Mitch smiled at him. "Nah, that's why we have you. You might think you're a bad penny, Reese, but you're sure turning out to be one cash cow for me. You can act as her mule in our area. We'll even make it look like you're selling the product so that she doesn't get too suspicious, and just maybe we'll get you enough in her good graces that we can learn the name of her cook. I'd love for the bitch to think she's pulled one over on us only to turn around and shove it in her face." Mitch stood and walked around the desk to sit in front of Reese. "See, as much as I'd like to crush Naomi like the rat she is, her cook is better than ours. If we can tell him the opportunities that he would get if he cooked for us instead, we wouldn't have to use too much force to run Naomi's shoddy business into the ground."

Reese frowned but said nothing. "So, it's not just undermining her on the dealing level? You want me to help you destroy her whole enterprise?"

Adam laughed behind Reese, the deep sound making his jump. Mitch clapped slowly as he shook his head. "Now you're getting it. There's always been a bit of bad blood between Naomi and me. Always thought she was better than me. I'm going to make sure that bitch knows where she belongs." Mitch leaned forward, his face inches away from Reese's, effectively pinning him to the chair. "But this is our little secret for now. If she asks you anything, you're none the wiser. Got it?"

Without waiting for a reply, Mitch smiled again and returned to his side of the desk, waving Reese away with his hand. Reese stood on shaky legs. Adam walked out beside him, mocking Reese for his slow realization of just how deep in he was.

It was late morning by the time Reese returned to his side of town. He habitually walked over to the garage despite it being the weekend. He had no desire to return to his apartment. It could burn with all of the things still left inside. There was little of himself in the apartment. Most of the items were just a carryover from his parents. Things that he'd stuck with because, in his heart, it still felt like theirs. Very little in there felt tied to him, and it held little sentimental value if it did. Why had he stayed all these years? He looked up at the business above the garage. He felt suddenly worn down by the life that he'd entrenched himself in. A life that had built up around him out of habit and a fear that looking for something different would show him that he was right where he was supposed to be. He still had the raise. He could stay at the garage, make a promise to himself that he would only stay there until he found something better. Something that fulfilled him and got him far away from Naomi, Mitch, or any of their plans for him.

Someone calling his name pulled him from his thoughts. He turned to see Millie Rae behind him. At that moment, she looked like the sun.

"What are you doing here so early?" he asked as he turned to face her. He hadn't meant to move closer to her, but he took her hand in his as he noticed her worried expression. "What's wrong?"

"I need your help."

Her worried expression didn't lift from her face as she moved to stand in his living room. She turned away from him, rubbing her hands along the backs of her arms.

Reese felt the tension peak inside him again as he took in what Millie Rae had said.

"What do you mean? Then why are you here?"

She grabbed his hands, and he was about to tell her what happened to him when he noticed that her hands were shaking.

"What's wrong?"

He followed Millie Rae to the back door of Rouge Palace. He tried not to shudder as she led him through the alleyway that had changed his life, but when he went up the cement steps into the dancer's entrance, he found himself overtaken by curiosity. The hallway off of the stage was a yellowed vinyl that emitted a heavy smell of smoke. The narrow corridor went to his right, where he could see numerous doors. The walls were covered in graffiti and scrawled signatures. Several pictures hung closer to the stage entrance, and Reese took a step towards them before Millie Rae grabbed his arm and yanked him down the hallway.

"Get in here. I don't need you gawking at everything," she snapped.

They passed an office and a large dressing room before coming to the second to last door. It was closed, but when Millie Rae opened it, he could see that it was a bathroom. It was larger than he had expected given the size of the backstage, but it still quickly became cramped as Millie Rae knelt on the floor, mopping the face of a young girl who lay limply in the bathtub. Forgetting his worries, ones he desperately wanted to share with Millie Rae, he quickly knelt behind Millie Rae and tried to catch what she was telling him in hushed tones.

"I shouldn't have encouraged her go to that other club," she was mumbling as she dabbed at the large bruise on the side of the younger girl's face with a washcloth.

The girl was shockingly pale. Reese could see the blue veins standing out on her neck and collarbones. He recognized her from around Rouge Palace; when he'd seen her, the girl had seemed fit and healthy, but the figure that lay before him was hardly the same person. In addition to the bruise on her face, Reese saw that her clothes were torn and filthy. Her feet were bare, the tights she wore had holes, and he could see the lime green nail polish on her toes. He saw her shoes sitting on the floor near the far end of the tub and realized Millie Rae must have taken them off. They were sneakers, making her seem that much younger. He figured seventeen at the most. He picked up the girl's hand and felt along the wrist for a pulse. It was there, but it was faint. He turned her hand over to look at the chipped nail polish, wondering if she had been in a fight when he saw the track marks on her arms. They were faint, a sign that she hadn't used in some time, but they made his blood run cold.

"What happened to her?" he asked quietly as he set the girl's hand back down next to her side.

Millie Rae shook her head and handed him the cloth she'd been using.

"Can you rinse that and bring it back warm? She's so cold, and I'm trying to get this dried blood off her face to see how bad the cut is. It's bruised and swollen so much I'm afraid she has a concussion."

Reese stood and quickly turned on the faucet, ringing out the washcloth as he did so. He rinsed the flecks of dried blood off the cloth as he waited for the water to warm.

"Not too hot," Millie Rae said from where she sat. "I don't want to hurt her more than she's already been hurt." She nodded to Reese as he handed her back the damp cloth. "Can you get me some blankets from the closet across the way? It's the last door on the right. They're old, but they're clean."

"Should we move her somewhere else?" Reese asked as he came back.

Millie Rae leaned back and sighed.

"I would if she'd wake up and do it on her own. She called me early this morning and told me to meet her. She came right in here and threw up. Said her head felt terrible. Obviously, with this goose egg, but when I checked on her, I found her passed out. I'm just worried it's a head injury. You aren't supposed to move people when they have a concussion, right? I figured it was better to keep her still."

Reese wasn't sure about telling Millie Rae that he thought people with head injuries weren't supposed to fall asleep either, but he kept his mouth shut and went to do her bidding. If she was already asleep, Reese didn't know how much good it would be to try and wake the girl up now. They tucked them around the girl's body, gently lifting her arms and legs to keep them away from the chill of the porcelain tub. Reese stood and watched as Millie Rae gently spent the next several minutes cleaning more of the girl's face. The girl's eyes languidly half-opened once or twice as Millie Rae moved the hair from her temple. Reese quickly had Millie Rae get a flashlight and shine it in the girl's eyes. Her pupils responded, although slightly sluggishly; Reese breathed a sigh of relief. Hopefully, nothing more than a minor concussion, and he told Millie Rae that the girl was probably safe to rest. Millie Rae stood and rinsed out the washcloth. She left it in the sink and shooed Reese out of the bathroom before turning off the light.

"Go on into the dressing room. I'll grab us something to drink."

The dressing room was lined with a long vanity and stage lights—makeup and bits of costumes strewn everywhere. Reese pulled a chair out and carefully set it around the discarded clothes. Millie Rae walked in and handed him a glass of water. She sighed at the mess and gathered some of the discarded clothes in her hand before tossing them up onto one of the empty chairs. She took a sip of her water before speaking.

"I need someone to watch her while I run over to her apartment and grab her things. I can take them to my house. She was going to move in with me anyhow. I really hope her head will heal on its own. I can't afford to take her to a doctor."

"Are you sure I should stay with her? What if she wakes up

confused? I doubt she'll recognize me."

Millie Rae frowned and nodded. "You're probably right. Damn." She drained her glass and leaned against the vanity, playing with a piece of jewelry left there. "It might just have to wait, and I doubt her roommate will let you in. I just didn't have anyone else to call, and I know that Mike would help, but he's out of town for the weekend. None of the other girls would have come this time of day. They're all sleeping. I just couldn't believe it when I saw you across the street."

"Is there anything else I can do?"

She shrugged, defeated.

"I can't go anywhere until she wakes up." She glanced outside the window before returning her gaze to him. She left her glass on the windowsill and stood, going over to sink into one of the beanbag chairs partially hidden behind a sliding rack of costumes. She patted the other one with her hand and gave him an enticingly over-the-top glance.

"Join me?"

Reese chuckled and went to sit down next to her. When he sank down, the bag was less stiff than he imagined, and he fell back into it, causing her to laugh. He sent her a grin and wriggled himself down into it to make himself comfortable.

"I haven't sat on one of these in ages."

"Glad I could change that for you." She leaned back into hers, flicking a speck of dust off the cloth. "These have been here forever, and it's not like anyone would cough up the money for a couch, but these just make the whole place seem discarded. Maybe because they look like colorful bags of trash." She shook her head and leaned back into the bean bag.

"Would you leave?" Reese had never thought about Millie Rae leaving the area, but he imagined that if prices kept rising in his neighborhood, it was bound to happen here as well, but she was shaking her head.

"I can't. At least, it doesn't feel like I can. If I'm struggling to stay here, it's not like there are many places that I could afford to move to. I live in my grandmother's house a couple of miles away. Left it to me after she passed. She'd been here for ages. Before the neighborhood got bad and the cheap apartments went up all around. She stayed in her nice house even though people originally couldn't stand the idea of a black woman in their area. Then, as the neighborhood became more diverse, the rich people ran for the country to get away from us. Then it was all we could do to move away from the area once the city said *we'd* made it run down. Now they're coming in and gentrifying it and acting like it's going to help improve the area, but all it's done is increase crime and show us once again that we're unwanted."

"So, you're staying out of love for a house and to spite the people coming in?"

"Damn right," she said, her mouth quirking as she looked at him out of the corner of her eye.

Reese smiled at her and played with a loose thread on the bean bag. "My parents never moved out of the apartment I now live in. I realize I don't like living there. I stayed there out of convenience. Now, I wish I'd run when I was young." He saw Millie Rae nod out of the corner of her eye. "Did your whole family live near here?"

"You're full of questions, hm?" She leaned up and rolled her neck. "My parents moved away. They said they wouldn't stay where they weren't wanted. When I decided not to follow my parent's or brother's career aspirations for me, I figured I had to make it on my own. I wanted to dance, so when my grandmother found out they weren't supporting me, she swooped in and offered her house. Said I could come here. Dance my little heart out."

"I could have guessed you were a dancer." He'd seen her move both on and off stage with the fluidity that suggested some training. What he didn't say anything about was how her passion for dancing landed her at Rouge Palace.

"Well, you're sweet. I stayed here after she died. Bounced around a few different studios, did pretty well until I was too old for the professionals. I considered teaching for a while, but I didn't like instructing. It didn't give me the same feeling. I landed at Rouge Palace, and I've been here ever since."

They sat in silence for a while until the back door banged open, and they both jumped. Reese blinked his dry eyes and realized he'd been dosing there on the bean bag next to Millie Rae. She quickly went to the hallway and glanced towards the entrance, a worried expression on her face. Reese stood, feeling as though he'd been caught doing something he shouldn't. Probably because customers weren't allowed to be back here, even if he helped tend an injured girl. Millie Rae's face smoothed into a smile, and she called a greeting down the hallway before turning back to Reese.

"It's one of the girls. She won't care if you're back here, but you should probably go." She walked Reese to the back door and hesitated before reaching out and hugging him. She put her hand on his face, and Reese felt his heart stutter to a stop. "Thank you. I don't know what I would have done." She dropped her hand. "Go home, Reese. You've earned some rest."

She closed the door behind him as he left, feeling better than he had in a long time.

Reese stayed home the rest of the weekend. He woke Monday

morning feeling invigorated. After pouring his tea into his thermos, he moved towards the front door but spotted the letter from the building manager that he hadn't paid attention to. He hesitated for a moment before picking it up and tucking it underneath his arm. He would read it after getting to work. The bounce in his step was something that he hadn't felt in a long time.

He began his morning rounds and was taken aback by the number of people who came up to him and said they'd heard about his job handling Lester and the break-in. They were thrilled he'd gotten a raise. He tried to focus on the smiles and congratulations he was receiving instead of being reminded that Lester could have very well been the dealer of Naomi's that had gone missing. Reese watched out for the man's telltale sand-colored car all morning, but it never showed. Reese was too terrified to ask around about it because he didn't want to hear an answer that confirmed his suspicions.

Sighing, he sat down with his tea and picked up the letter that had been stuffed under his apartment door this morning. It was short, with a secondary page behind it containing pricing. Reese read the letter feeling no love lost towards the landlord who had made his last weeks a living hell:

Residents,

I am writing to announce that a new agency is buying the apartment buildings I have tended for the past 50 years. I can no longer afford the upkeep of the buildings, and I did this for the best of the tenants. I will maintain the property until the next calendar month (30 days). After this time, you will be required to comply with the new company's pricing and policies, or you will be evicted.

Thank you for a wonderful 50 years.

Reese glared at the man's name signed hastily underneath his parting remark. Reese knew full well that the man had barely maintained the buildings. Reese also knew that the man had been itching to get rid of the property for ages. The only reason he was giving his tenants the regulated thirty days was most likely because the incoming company required it. He crumpled up the man's farewell note and threw it in the trash. He then turned to the official page from the new managing company and began reading that.

Cobblestone Complexes would like to welcome you to your new home! We desire to see our residents living in a complex that offers comfort and security in one of the fastest-growing areas in the city. We hope you'll welcome us into your hearts as we provide you with a safe place to rest your head. Pricing per apartment size can be found listed below.

Please know that we require the first and last payment, plus a security deposit for your apartment. We also require pay stubs from your work showing your monthly income. More details will follow in a detailed welcome packet, but please note that we must hear from you in thirty days to hold your spot. This area is in high demand, and these apartments won't last!

Reese didn't bother looking at the pricing. It would be far beyond his means. His slightly optimistic mood lay crumpled in the bin with the old building manager's resignation letter. He would be homeless. He knew that without a doubt. There was no way he could afford these new prices, even with his raise. He was suddenly blisteringly mad. The only reason these prices were so high was that people were moving into the area because it was up-and-coming. For people moving from nicer parts of the city, these prices were low, and they would have the advantage of being in an area that would only improve. It didn't matter that they were pushing people out of some of the only housing they could afford. He knew several tenants like himself that would be out of options when this new company came in. And they were only the first of many. Like the building that adjoined his garage, more businesses would move into the area because the land was cheap, and it was easier to build new. The more companies that came, the more people would demand housing in the area, further inflating prices, making the rising costs too demanding for people to swallow.

And how would people react? If they couldn't afford to live in an area, they'd have to move to find affordable housing, or they'd have to result to other means to get by. It was the same formula over and over again. Those with money would move into lower economic areas because the rent was cheaper but demanded all the comforts of where they lived. In the businesses would come, more than willing to accommodate an increase in demand. All of this under the glittering umbrella of progress, but without consideration of the already struggling people getting blinded by the onslaught.

Reese arrived home that night a great deal more bitter than he had left that morning. He took off his sweatshirt as he always did but, in a burst of anger, flung it on the ground and stamped on it rather than hang it as had been his custom. He suddenly hated the apartment he had spent the majority of his life in. He hated the yellowing walls, he hated the peeling, plastic counters, and he hated that this was his only option. He had no others. He wanted to shout. To slam his hands against the floor and let everyone know that he felt as if some great injustice had been done to him. He wanted to tear at the wallpaper, to blame his situation on anyone but himself. But he knew he was the only one he could blame. If he had only tried to better himself instead of taking the first job, he might have found himself a better life. People from high school had done it: gotten out. But he never had. And now, instead of raging against the apartment he'd lived in his entire life, instead of destroying the one place he'd called home, Reese simply sat on the floor and cried because he had nowhere else to go.

Chapter Nine

Reese slept fitfully that night. He surveyed the place in the morning and saw it again for the worn-down wreck that it was. He ran a hand down his face, instantly feeling the guilt creep in because it had been all his parents could afford, but the thought of leaving felt better than staying in the apartment when he knew that his time was short.

He went to the bedroom and pulled out a suitcase from the top of the closet. He packed quickly, tossing in only the things he used most frequently before moving to the bathroom to do the same thing. He felt suddenly detached from the space as if seeing it through another's eyes, and he saw how much of his parent's ghostly existence in the place still weighed on him.

In the kitchen, he collected his usual thermos, tucking it under one arm. He set the suitcase down on the small dining table and closed it. He slipped his jacket on, removed his key from the ring, and set it on the table. Closing the door, he walked down the rickety steps and felt a burden lift off his chest as he walked by the landlord. The man made a step towards him, but Reese felt no anxiety. The landlord glared at Reese before turning away.

Reese made his way to the garage and picked up a newspaper on the way to start looking for apartments. There had to be places that he was still able to afford in the area. He was jiggling the keys into the lock of the guard office when he saw Naomi's face in the reflection of the window pane.

He turned, his mouth and hands clenched tight. "You better

have a good reason for showing your face here. I could report you as a suspicious person, and you know that wouldn't be good for you."

She handed him an envelope, seeming unfazed by his threat. "There's information and money in there for a car sale. I want you to buy the car. Everything has to be by the books. Once you have the car, I'll tell you what you need to do from there." She smiled up at him. He felt his skin crawl. "You've been such a help, Reese; if I didn't have to blackmail you, you would be a great employee." She tapped her lip. "But maybe the threat of me harming Millie Rae is just the thing that makes you so effective."

Reese found nothing promising in the papers about apartments, so he found a cheap motel nearby that charged by the night. He tried to ignore the muffled moans and sounds coming from the room next to him as he sat on the bed. The springs crumpled under his weight, hardly even managing a squeak of protest. He opened the folder that Naomi had given him. The car was nondescript, and he imagined that was exactly why she wanted it. He found a slip of paper with a number on it and walked down to the front desk to use their phone.

"Hello."

"Hi, I'm calling about the car you have for sale."

"Hi, howdy, hey. Yep, it's still here, and it's wonderful. The wife and I love this car, but it's just not big enough for the grandkids. What kinda car you drive now?"

"None."

"Well, you can't do much better than this. Let me tell you, it's well-loved, but we've taken care of it. It's a bit high in miles, but she'll take good care of you."

"When can I come over to see it?"

Agreeing to meet in the morning, Reese took the bus to an

agreed-upon location to meet with the man. The grocery store's parking lot was reasonably vacant when Reese got there, and he looked around at all the buildings that looked newly built in the last few years. The bus ride had taken over an hour, and Reese couldn't quite believe the difference between his part of town and the one he now found himself in. There was hardly trash on the ground, and the people walking to and from the store all wore business attire. He saw several people get out alone from large SUVs. He waited in the far corner of the lot so that the man could find him. He'd given his description, and now that he could see where he was meeting the guy, he was regretting that decision. He stood out in his work clothes, and he had seen more than one person throw him a curious look before continuing on their way into the store.

The man drove up moments later in a forest green sedan. He stepped out and heartily shook Reese's hand. Reese opened up the hood and took a look at the oil and air filters while the man chatted happily behind him. Despite his wish to get away from this meeting with as little conversation as possible, Reese learned that the man and his wife had moved into a lovely house in an up-and-coming part of downtown. Because it wasn't in a large, established neighborhood, they'd been able to get the house for a great price. And wasn't it just great, but the four blocks surrounding their home had been bought out by builders so that they could put completely new constructions up where the old, dated houses had been.

Reese felt himself growing more and more irritated at this man each time he opened his mouth. That neighborhood hadn't been his, but it was only a little way away from where he had lived, and now all the people who had lived in those old, cheaper houses couldn't afford to stay. Sure, the builders had bought out the lots, but it meant rising prices for the surrounding area.

Reese offered the full asking price for the car.

The man seemed taken aback by the swiftness in Reese's decision, but since he was simply following orders, he hoped that it was overpriced simply to spite Naomi. The man agreed to a holding fee of ten percent of the car value. He'd get all the paperwork together and meet Reese later in the week to finish the sale. The man quickly took down Reese's information and gave Reese a handwritten receipt for the money given over.

Whatever Naomi's game was, Reese would figure it out. If it meant buying a car that looked on the edge of collapse, then so be it.

Reese told Naomi when he finally acquired the car later in the week. She gave him instructions on where to take the car. It was a garage he didn't recognize, but Reese drove the vehicle to the garage after acquiring the paperwork and keys. The garage was a fifty-minute drive outside the city, and Reese had never been out this far. He watched as the houses got more prominent and the properties grew. He passed several neighborhoods, but after some time, they faded away to a rural landscape. The houses each had character, and one of the connecting factors was the thin layer of dust that covered everything. The houses constantly seemed at war with the wilderness surrounding them. Some had staved off the overgrowth better than others, and when Reese pulled into the dirt driveway of one, he saw that the house had an oak tree leaning against the siding.

He parked the car by the garage and got out. He immediately noticed the difference in the air. It was dry, but it was clean, and he took a deep breath in. He closed the car door, not bothering to lock it, and walked up the cracked sidewalk to the entrance of the house. He knocked on the weather-beaten door, and he could hear shuffling inside. He had no idea who he would meet, but Naomi said that this was her contact. Reese was still in the dark as to who he would be working with, but he contorted his face to what he hoped was a neutral indifference and used the reflection in the glass cutout on the door to smooth his hair back from his face.

Despite hearing movement inside, no one had come to the door, and so Reese knocked harder this time. He knew someone was inside, and he didn't like being kept waiting.

"You can knock on that door all you want, but I ain't coming back inside so you can track dirt through my front room," a voice said from down the path he had just come.

Reese turned and saw an older man standing by the corner of the house. He had never seen someone look more like a caricature of a farmer in his life. The man's weather-beaten face was so profoundly wrinkled that he looked to be in a permanent scowl. His jeans were faded almost to white, and there were patches on the knees and the ends. His t-shirt had a faded beer advertisement on it, and the neck was frayed. There was a line around his head that Reese figured was from the near-permanent presence of a cap of some sort. His hair had a matching indentation everywhere the Reese could see. He had a pug nose that he wiped with the back of his hand. His hand looked to be covered in a thin layer of grease. He waved Reese towards him.

"You Naomi's new guy," he asked by way of introduction.

He didn't bother to shake Reese's hand but instead seemed to be holding out his hand for the keys to the car, which Reese gave to him. He turned away from Reese and walked back to the car before getting inside to pop the hood and trunk.

"Asked you a question," he prompted as he came back

around to the front of the car and began inspecting the engine.

Reese narrowed his eyes at the man's attitude. He certainly didn't like being treated like a delivery boy.

"I guess," was Reese's only answer.

The man nodded, seemingly satisfied with the response, and returned to the engine. Reese watched him work, wondering what he could learn about Naomi from this man. Nothing he had done up to this point had given him anything to go off, and the man seemed unwilling to say more than he had to. Reese folded his arms and looked around. Reese could see now that the tree wasn't leaning against the house. It might have at one point, but it looked like the man had taken a chainsaw to the leaning branches, so now only one half of the tree remained standing. The house seemed to sprawl away from the city, as if it was reveling in the extra space. It had been painted a pale green shade, but the paint was peeling in places. It didn't look to have a second story, but Reese could see a basement. He wondered what one man did with all that space, but the house didn't interest him beyond that. He shifted on his feet and wandered back towards the road. He could see the next house over and make out the small shape of a person working out in the garden. The distance between houses was so different from how people in the city constantly bombarded him. It felt strange to have so much space to himself. He could stretch out his arms and breath here. He wandered back towards the man, who had moved to the trunk and was pulling the spare out of the back.

Reese had never considered living this far out, not that he could make the commute into town every day, but he wondered what it would take to come out here and simply live. He pictured himself tending a garden like the person next door. Maybe Millie Rae would move out here with him. He took another deep breath of the clean air.

Reese wandered back past the tree and could see what looked like a tool shed and a secondary machine shed. Several older model cars similar to the one Reese had driven here sat parked to the side. He could see a stray cat rolling around underneath one. Having grown up his whole life in the city, Reese found the near silence of the rural setting unnerving. The space was liberating, but the silence was weighing on him. He didn't know if he could get used to simply listening to the leaves rustling.

"Have you lived out here long?" Reese asked as he walked back to the car.

The man simply grunted.

"How long have you known Naomi?" he asked, switching from meaningless questions to serious ones.

"A while."

The man straightened and threw the keys back to Reese. He barely caught them and clutched them to his chest. The man closed the trunk, having removed the spare from the back.

"Pull it around this way," the man gestured back towards the large machine shed.

Reese got in and started the car up. He pulled it around where he had been directed, keeping his eye out for anything that might give him a clue as to what Naomi had to do with this man. The man dumped the spare tire on top of what looked like a mountain of abandoned spares. Reese turned the car off and made to get out, but the man waved for him to stay. Reese desperately wanted to know what he was a part of, but he didn't want to seem overly eager, so he stayed where he was. The man disappeared around the corner and came back out, holding several black bags. He popped open the trunk, and Reese could feel the car move as the man removed the false bottom of the trunk and stashed the bags inside the space where the spare tire had sat moments before. Reese watched all this from the rear-view mirror. He'd have to get into the bags after he left the property. The man closed the trunk and came back around to the driver's side window.

"You know where you're meetin' her?"

"She didn't say," Reese confessed.

The man shook his head and pulled out his phone. He walked away, and Reese could tell he was angry by the way he gestured. The call was short, and when the man returned to the car, his already wrinkled face was pulled down in a harsher scowl.

"She said you'd meet her by the bridge five blocks south of the stadium tonight at eleven. Don't do nothing with the car. Just leave it as is. Park it in your garage or something. Just take it to her, and she'll do the rest."

Reese wanted to grab the man and demand more information from him, but he nodded and backed out of the shed. He pulled out of the driveway and started back down the road. The neighbor who had been gardening next door raised their hand in farewell. He saw the man watching him from his rear-view window, so Reese simply followed his directions back towards town.

Chapter Ten

He met Naomi where he'd been instructed, and he refused to leave the car until she walked around to the driver's door and dragged him from the vehicle. He watched as she distributed the drugs, hanging back by the car as she handed clear plastic bags of white powder to the men. She sent them on their way with a flick of her hand, and they faded into the scenery as quickly as they had appeared.

Naomi picked up what was left of the product and put it back in the trunk of Reese's car. She waved to Reese to get back in the car before surprising him and getting in the passenger seat herself.

"Drive south," she said without any other information.

It took everything in Reese to follow her direction. Even knowing that Mitch had done something to her dealer didn't make Reese feel more comfortable driving Naomi to his territory.

"Fuck this," Naomi said and smashed her phone against the dashboard of the car. Reese jumped, expecting more violence, but she smoothed out her hair and took a deep breath. "You drop me off. I don't want you coming in and fucking things up. You acting as a mole hasn't helped nearly at all, but I won't have your cover blown tonight. Stay in the car when we get there and make yourself useful by waiting."

The rest of the ride passed by in silence until they reached the house. Naomi let herself out of the car, slamming the door as she did so. She walked up the shadowed driveway and disappeared into the house. Reese strained his ears, honestly expecting to hear gunshots, but he found that more disturbing as the silence continued. Every rustle of grass and bark of a distant dog made him jump and glance towards the house. Naomi hadn't said how long to wait. No doubt she would want him to wait until she came out, but what if she never did?

The night dragged on, and despite his better judgment, Reese waited. He would rather wait until there was no doubt in his mind that she wasn't coming out than leave and face her wrath later. Still, as the minutes wore on, Reese rested his head on the headrest as he dozed. It amazed him that his eyes felt heavy. In such a situation, he would have thought himself unable to drift off, but he left his body simply shutting down from the stress that seemed to be attacking him from all angles.

The scuff of a shoe and the thunk of the car door opening jerked him into full wakefulness. Naomi was getting back in the car, her hand to her face. Reese couldn't see the damage right away, but when she flipped down the sun visor mirror and removed her hand, the light caught the wound in gashes of shadow and light. Her left eye looked swollen shut, but the gash on her forehead that was leaking blood down her jaw and onto the collar of her shirt looked ragged and frayed.

"Jesus," Reese said and frantically began looking around the car for something to hold against the wound.

"Stop your bitching," Naomi hissed as she pulled off her shirt, leaving only a camisole underneath. She wadded up her shirt and moaned as she held it to the wound. "I could have gotten worse, and you'd better not let him find out about you. They wouldn't even find your body." She waved her hand at him. "Get outta here." She closed the visor and leaned back.

"I should take you to the hospital."

Naomi snorted. "Not a chance. Hospitals ask too many questions. No, you'll take me to the farm and leave me there."

"That old man knows what to do with a wound like that?"

"I ask him or your girlfriend. I know she patches up the girls when the customers are too rough. I fully expect she'd trying to kill me if I was vulnerable around her, so yes, you'll drive me out to the farm and keep your mouth shut about the whole thing."

"I'm shocked he let you live," Reese said quietly after a few moments of silence.

"Honestly, me too, but the son-of-a-bitch knows how to push my buttons. Said he wouldn't destroy my entire operation if I brought him two shipments and delivered them to him personally. Mitch said that when he found out I had someone dealing on his turf he almost razed me to the ground without bothering to give me an explanation."

"I'm new to the drug dealing business, but it seems to me that dealing on someone else's turf is the first thing you learn not to do." He said it quietly, his hands tight on the steering wheel. "And that even letting you know you were about to get your operation destroyed seems rather—" He paused. "Gentlemanly, I guess."

"The only reason he has that turf is that my father thought it better to give it to a man rather than his daughter."

"And that's why he's nice?"

"The niceness is a mask. He wants to act like he's better than me. But let me ask you a question, Reese. Who would you rather put your chips on? Me or him?"

Reese said nothing, causing Naomi to laugh.

"That's the best answer you could have come up with."

Reese said nothing for several long moments.

"Why didn't you take over from your father?"

135

Naomi snorted, and he could see her turn to him from the corner of his eye. She was in shadow, but each time they passed under a light, it lit up her face for just a moment. The blood had seeped into the shirt some, making it look as though the wound was fountaining red.

"Whatever my dear uncle likes to think, being the apple of my father's eye did not equal me being worthy to take over for him." She laughed at Reese's grimace. "And maybe I was," she said this last part after a quiet pause. "I knew I could take over. I knew I could take the operation to a larger scale, build on the foundation he had set, but he wanted me to work in an office. I was supposed to be content with the life plan he set out for me. I couldn't expand the family business, but I sure could do my job to produce sons to take over eventually. I was written out of the picture because I didn't have a dick. I refused to be a pawn, so I tried to undermine him. Mitch? He was one of my father's distributors. I slept with him to get more information on my father's deals, but he turned on me. My father cut me off. Said if he saw me on his property again, he'd shoot me himself. He let that prick take over."

They turned into the driveway of the farm and parked in front of the garage.

"What will your father do when he learns you went to that house tonight?"

"My father died," she said. "Got cancer from smoking two packs a day. Went downhill fast. Mitch just keeps the threat going because he doesn't like that I tried to backstab him. Once they're both dead, I'll relish spitting on both their graves."

He shook himself and asked another question. "And your uncle? How does he fit?"

Naomi gently removed the shirt from her face and gently

touched the clotting blood at the wound site. "Bit dense, aren't you," she said. She waved her hand at the surrounding land.

"This is my uncle's place." She sighed. "My dad never thought the stuff my uncle made was good enough. Joke's on him; my uncle started making quality stuff for me after I came to him and said I wanted to run my father out of business." Naomi grinned, and it was lethal.

"So, you were dealing in his area out of spite," Reese said.

"Now you're getting it. I wanted a mule to deal in that area without Mitch's permission. Him being stupid enough to get caught by Mitch was his fault." She opened the door of the car but turned back to him before she stepped out. "Have a nice drive back to town, Reese." She slammed the door and walked towards the front door, where the outside light flickered in and out.

Reese didn't wait for her to go inside. He turned the car around and drove down to the end of the road before the stress of the night's events suddenly caught up with him, and he flung open the door of the car and threw up on the ground. He stayed there, head hung for a long while before wiping his mouth off and driving back towards town. Whatever mess he thought he'd gotten himself into paled now that he knew more about Naomi and Mitch's history. Naomi hadn't given up on her revenge in years, which meant that Reese would never be able to escape her. She'd asked him earlier which devil he'd rather lie with, and Reese wiped the sweat off his hands as he saw his options narrow into nothingness.

Chapter Eleven

Reese continued his drives to the farm at Naomi's instruction, and she kept him close during the distributions to the dealers. He knew it was simply because she had his balls on a string. Her words, and Reese knew she was right. He couldn't do anything to stand against her. Not the way things were going, and it made it all the worse when Naomi handed him a roll of cash one night. She said it was his cut.

He bought himself a decent meal for the first time in months with that cash. He took the car to a diner that he'd always thought was too far away and sat down for a meal. He tipped the waitress more than he would have been able to and pushed down the guilt that he might need that money later. The newness of having the extra cash in his wallet made him feel like a criminal as he walked out of the restaurant.

The motel he moved into that evening was better than his apartment, and when he handed his money over to the man at the front desk, the guilt that was riding him about spending the money became a smaller, sour pebble in his belly. It was nearly washed away with the warm shower and markedly more comfortable bed.

As he began to fall asleep that night, he looked up at the ceiling and wished that the lights of Rouge Palace were visible from where he lay, but he knew that they were far out of reach.

He doubted that Naomi was keeping up her end of the bargain and paying Millie Rae her full rate, so he always handed her any extra cash that he had from his cuts. No doubt the bartender kept tabs on everything happening in the place. He only visited when he was assigned, and the information that Mitch had fed to him kept Naomi happy.

He was driving by the building one morning, the window down in his car, when he saw a flash of white across the front of Rouge Palace. He slowed to see what the sign read, and what he saw made him swerve into the parking lot without a second thought. He got out of the car and walked to stand in front of it, the words a dark slash across the pieces of printer paper that had been taped together to make the sign.

"Closing after 20 years. Thanks for the support."

It had been thrown together with little care as the scotch tape holding it to the side of the building looked dried and reused. He reached up to touch the sign, wondering if pulling it down would reverse the fate of the place. He had no love for the business itself, for the illusion of comfort that it sold, but it was where he'd met Millie Rae. It was her livelihood, and his promise to try and keep her financially stable was torn from him as the weight of what the sign meant fully sank in. He went to the door and wrenched it open.

Despite the overpowering smell of cleaning products, Reese knew that nothing would be able to cut through the grime and dirt that had been crushed into the carpet over the many years of use. Reese knew that he had been drawn in by the lure of the neon lights out front, wondering what he would find inside. He had probably fallen for the false promises with more conviction than most, but he knew that Millie Rae was someone he could trust. He'd seen the character of some of the other girls. Knew they couldn't care whether the men came back or not. But Millie Rae wouldn't have offered him a place to live if she had cared so little for him.

Even though they weren't open, the girls he saw hanging by the bar didn't seem bothered by his presence. He walked up to one of the girls as she finished packing a cardboard box full of wrapped alcohol bottles. It took a moment, but he recognized her from the club. Without her makeup, she looked much younger than Reese could have guessed. Despite his concern for Millie Rae, he had to wonder what this girl would do now. Most likely, find another club to dance at.

Now that the neon lights were off all around the bar, Reese saw things tucked away that he usually wouldn't have noticed. Several pictures caught his eye, and he moved around the bar to get a closer look. In one of the pictures, Reese recognized a younger Millie Rae. She was maybe ten years younger than she was now, and he saw something in her eyes that made him reach forward and pick it up. There was a lightness there that he'd rarely seen when he visited her at the bar. Maybe it was the way her eyes crinkled up at the corners as she smiled. She stood to one side of an older man who had his arm slung around her shoulders. To the man's other side stood another young girl. She stood with her arm looped through the older man's arm and Reese could tell that the sharp cut of their faces related the man and this other girl.

Reese didn't recognize the location the picture was taken, but it must have been taken in the warmer months because both Millie Rae and the girl were in shorts and tank tops. Millie Rae and the man seemed genuinely happy in the picture, but the girl didn't, and Reese stared at the way her mouth pulled tightly to the side of her face for a moment before tucking the picture in his pocket. If it was his only photo of Millie Rae, he would hold onto it even if it wasn't his to take.

"Is Millie Rae in the back?" Reese asked the girl once he was done looking at the photos.

The girl shrugged and kept on wrapping the bottles. "She was earlier, but I don't know if she finished packing up her things."

He almost missed Millie Rae in one of the smaller rooms as he walked past. He turned around and hesitated by the door, wondering if she could tell he was there through the tulle and glitter. He saw the profile of her face almost trapped behind a colorful and flamboyant flurry of skirts. For a brief second, he saw her in a different time, as a dancer whose body was celebrated for its athleticism instead of the ability to sell sex. He could almost hear the music that would accompany the dances— the applause of the crowd.

"Listen, Millie Rae, I know you probably don't want me back here without— "

"I don't give a rat's ass why you're here, but you better help me with these damn things before I get strangled."

Reese's mouth opened in an "O" before he rushed forward and pulled a lemon-yellow skirt out into the hallway. The dress expanded into the space, and Reese saw that more colored skirts had taken up the area he had just liberated. Pushing the skirt to the side, he plunged back into the foray and struggled with more of the fabric. Reese reached for an emerald green material that seemed to wrap itself around him. He stepped back to struggle with it and felt Millie Rae's hands on his arms. They slid upwards, resting on his shoulders and her face was finally recognizable through one thin layer of material. Her lips touched his, their contact separated by the gauzy skirt before she pulled back.

Reese floated in a haze, wrapped in the skirt for a moment

141

more before struggling to pull himself free to face Millie Rae.

She had moved away by the time he was able to untangle himself from the cloth, and she seemed so entirely unchanged by what just happened that Reese feared he had somehow imagined the entire thing in the blink of an eye. Millie Rae glanced back at the dumbfounded look no doubt plastered on his face and shook her head.

"Stop gaping at me like a fish," she ordered before sighing.

"I don't understand. I had no idea that the place was closing. I thought I would have caught wind of it since so many of the businessmen visit here regularly." He gathered some skirts that she handed him and stuffed him into a waiting box in the hallway. "Do you need money? I have some saved up."

Millie Rae needn't know that the money was from the drugs he'd been dealing for Naomi, but he had a suspicion she knew where his windfall had come from.

"You've been generous enough, and I don't intend to wallow in the loss of my esteemed career." Her face broke with a smile that hinted to Reese how much the job had indeed been wearing her down.

"So, when did you all find out the place was changing ownership?"

She knelt and picked up the box of skirts she had finished packing. She jerked her chin at him so that he would follow her as they went back down the hallway to the front of the house. Reese watched her from behind for a while. She looked like she had lost a little weight. The cargo pants she wore were loose around her thighs, and he'd seen her wear those same pants before and complain about them being tight.

"We didn't know anything either. The manager called us all this morning and said it was free game if there was anything we wanted. Everything else is just going to be demolished."

He paused. "Demolished? They aren't going to use the building?"

They left the box on the stage and went back over to the bar. One of the girls gave them a couple of cans of light beer. Millie Rae opened hers, but Reese shook his head. He'd seen the girls drink often enough when they were working, but he'd have to get back over to the garage soon and couldn't follow suit. Millie Rae pulled up a chair at the bar. Reese remained standing and looked around at the space, which seemed more rundown in the daytime when the low lights didn't hide the more faded stains and years of wear.

"Guess not. I can't say I'm shocked they're tearing this place down. What with this place and the next lot over being bought out for office buildings and apartments, I would have brought this whole place down."

Millie Rae laughed when the girl behind the bar mimed swinging a bat at the bar then pointing finger guns towards the stage.

"I'm not sad to see it gone," the younger girl said. "It was getting close for me. I told myself I was gonna do this to pay the bills through school, but the money's so good that I almost thought about staying on after graduating. It was a good wake-up call."

"Maybe they'll build us a street-level bar, huh, Stacey? Have you seen those? People live, work, and eat all in one building. Like rats on a wheel."

The other girl laughed and opened another beer for herself.

"Those idiots don't know they've signed their lives over. Still, it might be nice. Maybe I'll apply for a management position with my degree, and when they ask what makes me want to work here, I'll tell them the truth. Anything is better than where I was working before." She laughed and rolled her eyes, but behind her bravado, Reese could see worry lines between her brows. "That'd send 'em for a loop." She put down her beer and piled her hair up on top of her head. "I bet they'd hire me if I lied and said I worked as a waitress while getting my degree."

The banter between the two melted away as Reese listened. He had nothing to add to the conversation, and that was fine with him. He was simply happy to be around Millie Rae.

He suddenly remembered the photo that he'd taken from the back of the bar and pulled it out of his pocket. He smoothed out the folds before tapping Millie Rae on the shoulder and showing it to her. She frowned for a moment, no doubt trying to place the picture, before she reached out a finger and tapped the face of the man.

"Now that's a face I haven't seen in years. His name was Johnathan. He was my first regular." She picked up the picture and flipped it over. Reese saw writing on the back, faded from years of sitting on the back of the bar. "Wow, this was a while ago. I must have been in my early twenties. I don't know the girl. I think it was his kid." She handed the photo back to Reese. "You can keep it. I don't care." She took a drink of her beer and turned back to the girl behind the bar.

Reese glanced at the clock behind the bar and sighed when he saw that he was ten minutes late for his shift. Pocketing the picture, he pulled out his wallet and handed Millie Rae half of the leftover cash from his last cut. She had said she didn't want it, but Reese set it down in front of her.

The girl leaned over and fanned the money out on the table.

"That's drug money. See the marker dots there up at the top? That's how Naomi marks them, so she knows if it ends up in the

144

wrong hands." The girl laughed as Millie Rae's face went ashy. "Oh, and I know she doesn't want you having that much money, Millie Rae. That woman has had it out for you since day one."

Reese glanced to Millie Rae, who stared at him with apparent dejection in her eyes. "I tell you how much I hate how she uses drugs to control the girls, and then you turn around and pay with that money?"

Reese shook his head. "Listen, things have gotten more complicated than I think you realized. Does it matter that it's Naomi's money? You need it. It's not like you have much of a choice."

Millie Rae stopped walking towards him. "Not much of a choice? I have a choice, Reese. I try to stay away from Naomi's corruption as much as possible. Keep the other girls away from being sold to far worse men than we get around here. All of that is my choice, but this," she points back towards the bills that sit on the counter. "That's you trying to take away my choice. From the beginning, you've wanted me to yourself. Don't try and deny it. You mistake me for that fantasy out on the sign out front." She runs her hand over her hair and shakes her head. "I thought you had a good heart, but I won't be bought out." She nods towards the door. "You know the way out. I don't want to see your face again."

Millie Rae turns and walks back towards the bar. She pushes the money onto the floor and heads towards the stage door, letting it slam shut behind her.

Chapter Twelve

Reese knocked on Stan's office door that afternoon. After the confrontation with Millie Rae, Reese had been too sick to go to work. He returned to the hotel and stared at the one picture he would probably ever have of Millie Rae. Faced with the reality that he had become precisely what Millie Rae had accused him of being, he had called Stan to set up a meeting to see how he might get Reese out of the situation.

After Stan let him inside, Reese poured himself a glass of water and came to sit in one of the chairs. Stan sat down across from him a moment later with a cup of coffee. They stared at each other for a few moments before Reese dropped his gaze to his pocket as he pulled out the picture.

Stan leaned forward and picked up the picture. He studied it front and back for a few moments before setting it back on the table. He folded his arms and studied Reese. As relieved to see that Stan was doing well, Reese felt a kernel of bitterness sit sour in his mouth at how calm Stan seemed about the situation. If Stan decided not to help him, Reese would be lost. He didn't think Stan would be that childish to hold a grudge for so long, but Reese had gotten himself into more trouble instead of finding a way out. Reese was walking a tightrope with coming to him.

He heard Stan stand up from his chair and move across the room. He heard a thump on the desk in front of him and looked up to see a cup of tea sitting there. He glanced over to Stan, who was moving back around to his side of the desk.

Stan searched Reese's face before sighing. "Let's talk about what's going on. You're drained, Reese, and seeing that you came here after I all but threatened to run you over with my truck speaks volumes." He folded his arms across his chest and adjusted to a more comfortable position in his chair. "Why don't you start from when I saw you last."

Reese told him everything, leaving nothing out, not caring if he repeated something from his frantic phone conversation the other night, all the while trying his best not to color his story with false details. He kept the time he spent with Millie Rae to a minimum simply because he couldn't bear it if Stan went to her with questions. He told Stan of the farmhouse, the car sale, and where Naomi had taken him the night they met Mitch. He ended with the picture, hoping that he had managed to remember everything. Hoping that Stan would have some way to help him.

"I don't know what to do," Reese said, ending his story.

Stan hadn't asked questions during Reese's tale. He had taken a series of notes, which he looked at now, grinding his teeth together as he did so.

"You don't want to go to the cops because of your crimes?"

Reese nodded. "I'm sure I'd still get thrown in jail."

"You probably would," Stan said, not bothering to steer Reese away from the truth. "I can find out what I can about her from my contacts at the police, but my hands are tied. I don't have that kind of authority to do anything." Stan leaned back and drummed his fingers against his desk. "I honestly wish I could help you, but I'm not a cop any more. Maybe when I talk to them, we can work out some leniency for you, but I have a feeling you're in too deep to get out clean."

Reese tried not to wince at Stan's assessment of his situation, even though he knew it was true.

"My unprofessional opinion," Stan continued, "is to keep doing what you're doing. Stay relevant, but don't ask questions. I'll find out what I can on my own." He turned on his computer and quickly pulled up his calendar. "I can maybe get you some information this upcoming week, depending on how long it takes me to get in contact. When is your next drop with her?"

"I'm not sure," Reese said. "She only calls me when she needs me."

Stan nodded, stood, and gestured for Reese to follow him to the door. Stan hesitated as he opened it, clapping Reese's shoulder.

"I'll call you at the hotel if I find something."

"What can I do?"

Stan stared at him for a few moments, and Reese wondered if he could see a flicker of worry in Stan's eyes.

"Keep your head down."

Reese had a message waiting for him at the hotel when he got back late that night. The man at the front desk handed it over, never taking his gaze away from the book he held. Reese didn't bother thanking him. He had little doubt that it was Naomi contacting him. He opened the door to his room and threw the convenience store bag on the bed before sinking down next to it. He opened the slip of paper, saw Naomi's name, and picked up the phone to call her. He lay back on the bed, the cord pulled taut across his belly, and thought about not answering her summons. He could simply leave the area, but he'd seen how vengeful she could be. Even if he kept her operation a secret, he knew he could never return to the area. He resigned himself to playing his part and dialed his number. She answered on the first ring.

"Where the fuck have you been?"

Reese sat up, the anger nearly palpable through the phone. He swallowed nervously; he'd never heard her swear before. "I was out," he answered. "What do you need?"

"I need you to be around when I call. Meet me at the corner train station on the south end of town. Wait for me there." The line clicked shut.

Reese didn't waste any time, and it wasn't for Naomi's sake that he hurried. If he took longer getting there than she deemed appropriate, he had no idea what she'd do to him. The drive there was tense, but he found the station and parked the car under a light pole so that she could see him. He waited around inside the car, but when she didn't show up after several minutes, he got out and walked to the edge of the light. He walked around the edge for a few moments, always trying to stay in the light so that she could see him, but she didn't appear.

Finally, growing tired of waiting, he locked the car and stepped into the darkened street to look for her. There was at least a ten-minute drive from here to Mitch's house, so he doubted she would have walked from here to there. Her urgency on the phone, coupled with her absence at their meeting spot, had him worried. He ran a hand over his face and looked up and down the street before turning and walking down the road towards the businesses.

None were open, but the lights from their neon signs gave him a sense of protection. He didn't like this area of town. He liked it less after learning this was where Naomi had come from. He trudged past several closed storefronts before pausing to listen for any sound that might indicate she was near. He heard nothing. The silence felt as if it were crawling up the back of his neck to rest heavily on his shoulders. He could tell that something wasn't right with the area. It was as if it were alive. The whole place was crouched, waiting to see what would happen next. He quickly turned and walked back towards the car. He didn't care if Naomi was walking around the place all night. He wasn't about to go looking for her.

He sighed when he saw Naomi leaning against the car's hood when he rounded the corner to the parking lot. Her thin figure seemed to be folding in on itself. Her casual clothes seemed at odds with what Reese had seen her wear every other time he'd been around her, and he had to wonder why she was down here at this time of night. He frowned, realizing the strangeness at which she sat contrasted with her agitated tone earlier. Reese lengthened his stride as he drew closer, and he could see that one hand was holding her side. In the yellow light of the streetlamp, he could see the parts of her face that weren't sporting a massive bruise had a sheen to it that made her look like a wax doll.

"Naomi, I was looking for you," he said as he reached her. He stopped when he saw the blood between her fingers and realized why she had been holding her side so awkwardly. "What the hell?" His hands reached out to help her, but she waved him away.

"If you had gotten here when I first tried to call you, this wouldn't be an issue," she said with a forced aggressiveness. Her face was pale, sweat beaded on her brow, and her breathing was shallow.

His hands hovered around her anxiously as he scanned the area, looking to see if anyone had followed them here.

"We need to get you to a hospital this time. Who did this to you?"

"I was trying to even the playing field with Mitch. He didn't like me trying to sell him inferior product made to look like my uncle's. Go ahead and take a wild ass guess what happened." She laughed softly and shook her head. "All hospitals have to report gunshot wounds, you idiot. I'm not getting help."

Reese knelt down to get a better look at the wound. The blood was slowly seeping through her fingers and staining the front of her shirt. He quickly unbound his flannel shirt and shoved it at her. "Use that instead of your hand."

She reached out, the pain making her slow, and held the shirt to her stomach. She looked up at him, and Reese saw tears forming in her eyes.

"And what good is this going to do me?" Frantic terror crept into her voice. She bent over herself and cried softly at the pain. "I have nowhere to go," she said, her voice rising in pitch.

Reese grabbed her shoulder before she could slide off the side of the car and helped her around the car to the passenger side.

"We're going to get you help," he said as he took most of her weight and slid her into the seat. She sank down, leaving a streak of blood on the seat and door. She wailed into his shoulder as he bent over and moved her legs into the car.

"Just let me die if this is what you're helping feels like," she said, leaning back against the headrest and panting. "I'm fucking shot, and you can't even be gentle with me. I fucking hate you."

He saw her swallow heavily before opening her eyes and turning to look at him.

"You take my bag. Don't get your prints on it. Throw it away. Report the car stolen as soon as you get back to the hotel room."

He shut the door carefully, ignored her request, and grabbed her bag as he walked around the front of the car before getting in and throwing her purse in the back. He started the car and tried

151

not to breathe too heavily as the smell of her blood mixed with the scent of the car. He scanned the area once more, fully expecting to see dark figures moving in to finish the job, but he saw nothing as he pulled away from the parking lot.

He got onto the highway and sped towards the farmhouse. It was his only option, and he hoped that the old man would be willing to help if only because Naomi was his niece. He glanced over to her and saw that her eyes had closed, her head hung down on her chest, her usually thin face appearing more skeletal due to the waxy whiteness of her skin. Reese reached over and put his fingers on her wrist. He could feel her pulse, but just barely. This was the only thing he would do to help her. Having her go to the hospital would endanger him as well.

He started flashing his lights and honking his horn as soon as he turned into the driveway for the farmhouse. He hit a pothole in the dirt road, and Naomi groaned at the motion. The man approached the moving car, but Reese didn't stop until he pulled into the drive. Getting out, he went around to the other side of the car. Reese opened the passenger door and checked Naomi's stomach. His shirt was decently wet, and his hand was bloody where he'd touched her. He heard the man cursing and telling him to move. Reese got out of the way as the man knelt and picked Naomi up with surprising gentleness.

They headed back to the house, and Reese held the various doors open until they reached a bedroom and set her down. Naomi hadn't said anything as she'd been carried inside, but her eyes flickered open briefly before shutting again.

The man pulled Reese's shirt from the wound and threw it to the other side of the bed. Gently, he peeled Naomi's shirt away from her stomach. The wound was bleeding sluggishly, the skin torn and frayed. Reese felt bile rise in his throat, so he left the

152

room and quickly searched for towels and antiseptic in the bathroom across the hall. The man promptly left the room and walked past him a moment later, carrying a bowl with water in it. Reese could hear the trickling of water from where he was in the bathroom and then the squeak of bedsprings as the man most likely sat down next to Naomi to begin cleaning her wound.

He found some iodine, ace bandages, and some gauze, which he carried into the other room. He knew none of this would be a lasting solution for the gunshot, but it would hopefully be enough to keep her alive until they could develop a better treatment.

"What happened?" the man asked as he wiped away more blood from the wound and carefully cleaned around it with iodine.

"She called me earlier. She wanted me to come get her. She was in Mitch's territory. She got shot."

The man's hands stilled for a moment, but they quickly picked up the pace once more as he started packing the wound with the gauze Reese had found. He gestured behind him with a bloody hand. "Start soaking those in iodine and handing them to me. I don't even know if this'll work. She's still bleeding. Think you're supposed to wait until after it stops, but I need to get this wrapped up."

Reese could tell that he was talking more to himself, so he simply did as he was asked. He handed the man pad after pad soaked in the medicine. Reese had no idea how long they sat there, running through the meager supplies with frightening speed. He only knew Naomi was alive because she would occasionally groan, earning words of encouragement from her uncle. They moved to the ace bandages to hold everything in place and secured them with a little metal butterfly clasp.

The man stood and moved past Reese. His hands were

covered in a mixture of blood and iodine. Dried blood caked around his elbows, and newer, fresh blood glistened on his fingers. Reese heard the water run from the bathroom for a moment before he turned away from Naomi and went to join the other man.

"She didn't want to go to a hospital," Reese said by way of apology and explanation.

"No, she wouldn't have," he said, and Reese felt relieved that perhaps he had done the right thing.

The man pumped more soap into his hands, the water running a bloody brown down the drain. He scrubbed vigorously with his nails at the dried residue up at the top of his arms.

"The bullet is still inside her," Reese said. He glanced back toward the room where Naomi lay. Reese knew that it was worse that there wasn't an exit wound. They had trapped the bullet inside Naomi's body, but they didn't have the tools to get it out. Reese didn't want to think about what that meant for her in the long run. They had no way of knowing whether she'd make it through the night.

Chapter Thirteen

Reese hardly slept that night. He and the man broke the night up into four-hour shifts, checking on her every half hour. Her pulse dipped low as the sun came up, but she seemed to grow stronger as the light came fully into her room. She opened her eyes when Reese checked on her once, and he took that awareness as a good sign.

The man brewed him coffee, which Reese accepted for the first time in his life. He took a single sip and decided that it was to be his only cup of coffee. He doubted the man would have noticed if he hadn't finished it, but then it was the only kind thing he could do for him. Reese had brought his niece to him, bleeding from the gut. The least he could do was take the cup of coffee without complaint.

They let Naomi sleep through the afternoon but decided to wake her up to try and get her to drink something. She only spat it up, coughing as she did and reopening her wound. They bandaged it up and didn't try again. Reese sat by her side for several hours after that, afraid the stress would be too much, and she had slipped back into a deep sleep, but beyond that, she didn't seem any worse.

After their attempt to give Naomi something to drink, the man had left the house, and Reese could hear banging from the machine shed. Whether he was taking out his frustration or building something to help, Reese didn't know, and he wasn't going to risk his skin to go and check. Reese traced the pattern in the comforter that Naomi lay on and listened to the banging outside for as long as he could stand.

He finally stood as the sun was setting and walked out to the machine shed. The banging had stopped a while ago, and Reese needed to talk to the man. He had no idea what to do next, but he needed to get back into town. He needed to see if repercussions had happened from the attack on Naomi.

"I need to borrow one of your cars," Reese said when the man saw him coming into the shed.

The man nodded, turning away from Reese to dig into the shelf next to him. He tossed Reese a set of keys. "It goes to that truck." He gestured to a small, outdated truck. "You best do something about your car before you leave. It can't be taken anywhere. It'll cause too many questions with the inside looking like it does."

Reese tucked the keys in his pocket and glanced back to the car he'd driven to the farm last night.

"And what do you suggest I do with the car?"

The man crossed his arms. He had been helpful until this point, but Reese wondered if he would force Reese to figure this out himself. He hoped not. Finally, he spoke.

"I'd take the plates off the car. Scratch out the VIN, and pull out anything of yours you might have in the glove box. No point in cleaning the blood off. Anyhow, there's an abandoned factory down the road. No one goes there." He gestured out past his house to where the factory must lay in the distance. "You take it out there and light it up. That should burn any evidence out of it, and since you're taking the plates off and such, we should be fine."

Reese stared at the man for some time. Reese had known the man wasn't fazed by breaking the law, but his easy solution for

156

getting rid of the car had Reese wondering if the man hadn't used the same tactic before.

"When do you want to leave to do this?"

The man stared at him for several long moments before his jaw jutted forward.

"You think I don't have stuff around here to do?" he yelled. "You want me to hold your hand and help you clean up your mess? You shit head. I should let you rot for what happened to Naomi."

He lunged at Reese and grabbed him by his shirt.

"You're doing this on your own, and don't expect my help no more." He shook Reese to emphasize his point. "You take that car and get out of here. You'll walk your ass back here after you're done. You can keep that truck for all I care." He shoved Reese away, and Reese wondered if the man would come at him again. Instead, he seemed to crumple in on himself. "I gotta stay here with Naomi. Even an idiot like yourself must realize she don't have much time left."

Reese left him then, feeling ashamed because he seemed like someone who was only doing the best he could. He went back inside the house and picked up the car keys off the kitchen counter. He stopped in briefly to check on Naomi and saw that she was still sleeping.

Reese drove the car out towards the direction the old man had pointed. It was foolish, but he hadn't asked for any more directions, afraid the man would simply chase him off his property. He kept the windows rolled down and welcomed the cooler air as it chased away the smell of blood that still lingered in the car. He'd gathered a gas can and a lighter from the man's garage before leaving. He didn't bother asking for them. The man had watched him take them and had said nothing. Reese's palms were sweating at the thought that he wouldn't find the place with the man's limited directions, but just as he was flicking on his headlights, he saw looming stacks of concrete in the distance. He sped towards them, relieved that he had found them, and pulled into the drive.

Now that he was closer, he could see the tall buildings were large grain silos. A conveyor belt reached the top of the silo, the base attached to the largest building where the grain must have been cleaned. He pulled around the back and relaxed when he saw that all the doors were chained shut. Reese had worried that people would still be lurking around the business. Even drifters would notice a guy pulling in to burn a car, but he didn't see signs of anyone.

He got out of the car and looked around the place, trying to find the best resting place for the vehicle. He walked towards the building and looked in several of the windows. Dust and dirt had piled up on the inside, and he could still see sacks of grain that looked as though they were left half-filled. Despite the somberness, Reese had to admit he liked the stillness of the place. The quiet was immense around him, and he realized how much noise had been bouncing around in his head. The city noise, the noise of his thoughts, and the noise of his conscious weighed on Reese.

He just wanted to stay here. To stay in this abandoned place and abandon his problems here so he wouldn't have to deal with them anymore. He would leave behind the theft, the lying, the drugs, and watch over this place until both he and it crumbled into dust. It was tempting—to leave all of his problems behind—and not have to deal with the consequences. He still resented Naomi for how she'd pulled him into helping her, but when he'd seen her in pain, he realized that she was just another person, dark history or not. Still, things had gotten so messed up that he didn't know what the right choice was now. Once he headed back to town, he had no idea what he should do.

He wiped away the dust from the window on his pants and walked back to the car. He got inside and turned it on, opening all the doors and letting the thing run itself out of gas. He'd hide the evidence, but he didn't want it exploding and bringing unwanted attention. He sat on the ground next to the gas can he'd pulled out of the car and waited until it died. It took longer than he had expected, and it was nearly full dark by the time the car died. Reese went back into the car and found the flashlight he threw in at the last minute. Holding it in one hand, he struggled to scratch away some of the VIN. He didn't get it all, but he hoped the fire would take care of the rest of it. He moved around to the front of the car and groaned.

He had forgotten a screwdriver. He almost considered giving up then and there, but he found the plates weren't as tight as he thought. He was able to get the front plate off relatively quickly by loosening the screws with his fingers. He tossed the plate over by the gas can and went around to the back. This one was stuck, and he struggled with it for several minutes, growing more and more frustrated as he didn't get any closer to success.

He wiped his now sweaty hands on his pants and tried once more before finally grabbing the plate and jerking on it several times. He yelped as the metal gave away, the force of his pull flinging him back as the plate split. The sharp metal cut deep into the soft flesh of his palm as he fell backwards. He lay on the ground for several moments, cradling his palm to his chest as the pain radiated up his arm. He glared at the split plate that now sat on the ground and kicked it away in anger.

The darkness that had moments before been a blessing now felt like it was hiding sinister forces. Reese shook his head, trying to dislodge the thoughts, and pulled off his plaid shirt and undershirt. He wrapped his bloody hand in the undershirt, struggling to tie it with only one hand, and slipped the warmer of the two items back over his shoulders. He got the essential buttons done before walking over to the gas can.

He poured the fluid everywhere, even opening up the trunk and hood to pour gas inside. He got the tires and the roof but put most of it on the stains where Naomi had sat the night before. He momentarily wondered if an old car was like old kindling. The older and drier the kindling, the easier it would catch and burn. Reese hoped so. He poured the last few drops on the backseat and set the can down well away from the car. He had thought about just tossing that in and not bothering to carry it back, but he didn't need the man having any more reasons to hate him.

He pulled out the lighter and flicked it into flame. He simply watched it for a few moments, enjoying the heat and light it gave off. He threw it into the car and quickly took several steps back.

It lit quickly, for that he was grateful, and he watched it for some time, taking in the heat and the light as it chased away the encroaching shadows and chill. He lingered, making sure that the evidence would be destroyed, or at least muddled should anyone have the desire to search the burned car.

He bent and gathered the things he would take back to the farm. He tucked the license plate under the arm with the injured hand, picked up the can, and turned on the flashlight.

He walked away from the still blazing car, not caring if any embers touched the nearby building and sent it up in flame. He'd done his job, and now he just wanted to get back to the house and check on Naomi. It would take him several hours to get back to the house. The old factory had been a decent thirty-minute drive away from the house, and he didn't appreciate having to walk back in the dark along the side of the road. He wasn't concerned about getting hit. He hadn't seen any cars pass by him on the way to the factory, and now that the sun had set, he doubted anyone would be coming out this way.

It left him alone with his thoughts on a long road. His flashlight bounced with his footsteps, and he found a rhythm that suited him. He realized that he missed walking. He hadn't walked nearly as much since he'd moved away from the apartment. When he'd been there, he'd walked everywhere, and there was a certain freedom in that. He could go where he wanted, but with driving a car, he felt limited. For so many, a car spoke of freedom. Of the ability to travel long distances, see new things. Reese had seen so much since he started driving for Naomi, and none of it had been good.

His mind turned back towards Naomi as the darkness fully descended on him. He could still label his feelings toward her as negative, but the hate had gone out of him when he'd seen her struggling. There was no love lost between them, but he'd seen her fear of being shot, seen the rage and frustration at not being able to go through with her plan. It made her human in his eyes. Still, he didn't plan on helping her any more. As far as they were concerned, he had helped her to the farmhouse. Any debt he owed her was paid in full. And she wouldn't be able to find him if he chose to disappear.

Oh, how he wanted to disappear. He wanted to put this all behind him. To look at his past year's actions and say that it was a chain of events that happened outside of his control. He knew that wasn't the truth, as much as he would have liked to believe otherwise, but if he said it often enough and with enough

161

conviction, it would become his truth.

He finally turned down the road towards the old farmhouse, and he was grateful that the man had left the lights on. Maybe he could convince the man to patch him up. He figured the man would rather see him freeze on his doorstep, but the man kept grudgingly helping him when Reese asked. He imagined it was because of his association with Naomi, and he'd only have to push his luck this one last time.

He trudged up the stairs and opened the door. The warmth of the house hit him squarely in the forehead and made him startlingly aware of the pain coming from his hand.

He didn't see the man in the front room, so he headed back towards the guest room and was astonished when he saw that Naomi's eyes were open.

Chapter Fourteen

Reese quickly forgot about his injury and went over to the bed. She watched him walk in, but she didn't say anything. He couldn't imagine the pain she must be in, and he doubted the man had any medicine strong enough to keep the pain at bay. He sat down on the edge of the bed but got up right away when he saw her wince at the movement.

"Sorry," he said. "Does your uncle know you're awake?"

She nodded. Reese doubted she would want to try and speak. Even breathing must be painful with the wound to her stomach.

"Have you been awake long?" he asked and found himself whispering as if the volume of his voice would change how much pain she was in.

Again, she shook her head. She held her hand out in the air and pinched her fingers together. She moved her arm up and down, slowly moving from left to right, and Reese frowned at her.

"What? Oh, do you want something to write on?"

Her eyes rolled upwards, and he imagined she would have hit him, given a chance. He quickly searched around for a piece of paper and a pen. He found both in the kitchen and hurried back into the room. He set both down on the bed beside her and pulled a chair up to the bed. Naomi quickly scratched out a few lines of questions and handed them to Reese.

"Ah, let's see. I brought you here last night. You've been asleep for most of that. I don't know when you woke up. I haven't seen or heard anything from Mitch, but I haven't driven back into town. Yes, your uncle knows who did it. He hasn't said anything else to me. My hand? Oh, I cut it open making sure the car was taken care of." Reese handed her back the paper, and she scribbled more questions on it. She handed it back to him. "Yes, I'm an idiot. 'Was your uncle angry when he heard it was Mitch?' I don't know. I think he was generally pissed off that you got shot." She grabbed the piece of paper and wrote frantically again. Reese frowned as her breathing became more labored as she struggled to write. "Why don't you take a break? You don't want to overdo it." He reached for the paper, but she jerked it away, groaning as the movement pulled at her bandages. She sighed and nodded, handing him the paper.

Reese put it on the bedside table and went to grab her a glass of water. She drank in little sips, only finishing a third of the glass before she pushed it away. There were deep purple bags under her eyes, and Reese thought she almost looked worse now that she was awake. He helped her get into a better sleeping position before pulling up her shirt and looking at the bandage. It looked as though her uncle had changed the dressing while Reese had been gone. The new bandage was slightly smaller and seemed to have less padding, which Reese considered a good sign. He pulled her shirt down and pulled the blanket back up. He turned off the light as he walked out and shut the door behind him.

He went searching for Naomi's uncle and found him in the kitchen. He had no idea where the man had been, but now he stood drinking a beer in front of the sink.

"Thought I said I didn't want to see you again," he said as he watched Reese come into the kitchen.

Reese nodded, not feeling like responding. He began unwrapping his hand; the pain was finally unbearable now that

164

Reese had nothing else to focus on. He sensed the man watching him, but he stayed silent. In the light, the cut wasn't as bad as he'd thought. It was a long cut, but it wasn't as deep as he'd initially thought. It started at the fleshiest part of his palm and arced upwards toward the bones of his pointer finger. The skin was shredded, and he knew that it wouldn't be fixable this way. The sides would have to be smooth to stitch across it. He turned the faucet on and gently ran his hand underneath it. The bleeding had caked over most of the wound, a dark red worm that held his flesh together. The water turned pink as he rinsed off the blood that had dried around his makeshift t-shirt bandage.

As Reese was cleaning his hand, the man moved away and came back moments later with more gauze and tape. He set them on the counter next to Reese and took another drink of his beer.

"You could get stitches for that. Hospital won't think nothing of a guy ripping his hand open doing work on a car."

"Work on a car," Reese repeated, looking at his hand and seeing all that had led up to the wound. Surely, they would know; his numerous guilty actions had been stacking higher and higher so that by now, someone must notice that they hung like a noose around his neck.

Reese heard the man sigh behind him. "You want to tell them the truth? That you cut it open because you were burning evidence? No, so you lie and say you were working on a car. Simple as that."

"I still need your truck. Naomi wants me to check in on some things," he said.

"She's a micromanaging bitch is what she is," the man said, anger making his words short and curt.

The man's language surprised Reese, but he kept that to himself. The man cared deeply for his niece, but Reese couldn't deny that her nature had made her walk into dangerous territory. It was her fault she'd been injured in the first place. Reese could sense the man's language came from his fear and anger that Naomi had been hurt, though he couldn't disagree that Naomi was anything but micromanaging.

Reese finished bandaging up his hand and turned around to face the man. He was leaning against the opposite counter, his arms crossed, his face in a deep scowl.

"I'll leave tonight, but I'll be back to report to Naomi."

"You tell me if you hear anything about that shit head Mitch. I'm liable to head down there myself and beat him to a pulp."

Reese felt his eyebrows raise almost up to his hairline. "I didn't realize you knew much about Mitch other than he was Naomi's competition."

The man grabbed another beer and popped it open. "Oh, I know more about their history than I care to admit." He took several deep drinks of his beer before continuing. "Naomi's daddy, my brother, didn't think my product was good enough. When Mitch took over, he snubbed me just because that's the way it was. Naomi and I both have reasons to hate that prick."

Reese nodded, putting that information in the back of his mind for later use. He flexed his hand slowly, figuring out his range of motion before nodding to the man and heading for the door. He opened it but turned back one last time to see the man's back. "I'll stop by in the next couple of days if I don't hear from you." He saw the man nod and took that as a sign that he might not shoot him upon his arrival. He shut the door behind him and headed for the truck.

Reese got into town without realizing the stereo was on. He was so lost in his thoughts that the noise of his mind had overpowered

166

the music bouncing around the cab of the truck. He pulled into the parking lot of his motel room and switched off the truck. A new person sat at the desk when he stopped in to ask if he had any notes delivered. This time, it was a young man, and he popped his gum as he sorted through the messages.

"You got a couple," he said, handing Reese a little stack of sticky notes with phone numbers on them. "One guy came by a couple of times and asked for you."

Reese thanked him and took the papers back to his room. He recognized one number as being Millie Rae's and one as Stan's. The last number was unknown to him. It was late enough that he didn't bother dialing any of them right now. He sat down on the bed, the gravity of his exhaustion and stress of the situation fully settling on his shoulders. He lay down, hoping to distribute the weight throughout his whole body. He finally fell asleep as he was, still dressed in his clothes from several days ago.

He called Millie Rae's house the following day and left a message apologizing for missing her call. He said nothing more as an explanation but said he'd very much like to meet her at the diner for dinner that night so that he could better explain himself. He ignored the number that he didn't recognize and instead dialed Stan's number. Reese felt clammy as he listened to the phone ring, thinking that Stan must have found something of importance to call him before their scheduled meeting the following week. Stan finally picked up on the third ring.

"Stan here."

"It's Reese, look—"

"Shit, man. Where have you been? I've been trying to get a hold of you. Look, don't say anything over the phone. You're at your hotel room?"

"Ah, yes."

"I'll be there in fifteen minutes." The line clicked, and Reese frowned at the receiver in his hands.

Reese tried to walk down to the lobby, where the hotel served a continental breakfast on the weekdays, but he felt so frazzled by the urgency in Stan's voice that he simply went back to his room with a cup of tea. Secretly, Reese had been hoping that Stan had been calling to check in. The events with Naomi, coupled with Stan's phone calls, did not sit well with Reese. Reese was thankful he'd told Stan everything up until this last chain of events. It would simply be too hard for Reese to untangle everything at this point. He paced back and forth in his room, waiting for Stan.

The urgent knock sounded at his door ten minutes later, and Reese checked to make sure it was Stan before opening the door.

"I thought you said fifteen minutes," Reese said, hoping his levity would remove the scowl on Stan's face.

"I sped," Stan said as he came into the room and sat down in the chair by the desk.

He fixed Reese with a look that didn't waver, and Reese wondered momentarily if he should be apologizing for something.

"Where have you been, Reese? I've tried to call you here several times, and I drove by the garage. Some guy I talked to said you hadn't been in for several days. I don't know if that job will be waiting for you when you go back."

Reese sank onto the bed and put his hands on his knees. He saw Stan's eyes narrow in on the bandage still around his hand.

"You better tell me what's going on right now."

Reese sighed and ran his good hand over his face. "Well, Naomi went to see Mitch. Said she was trying to even the playing field. She got shot." He held up his hand as Stan opened his mouth to question him. "Let me finish. She called me after to come and get her. I drove her to get help. She wouldn't let me take her to a hospital. The person I took her to got her patched up, but I don't think she'll last more than a week or so without proper treatment."

Stan sat back in his chair, silent for some time. His leg jiggled frantically as if his mind's need to think quietly warred with his body's need to pace. Reese waited for a few moments, thinking Stan would offer some advice, but when he remained silent longer than Reese could stand, he got up and went to the bathroom to check on his wound.

"Here's the way I see it," Stan said from where he sat. "You're in deep shit. Deeper shit because you helped Naomi. You're an accessory. I've been researching her father. That man was nasty. Suspected of killing her mother, but he wasn't charged for it. And drugs were the tip of the iceberg for him. Human trafficking seemed to be his preferred money maker. It seems like he owned the club before Naomi bought it after his death."

Reese came out of the bathroom, his face pale. "He owned that?"

Stan nodded. "Up until he died."

Reese felt the blood drain from his face, and he sagged onto the bed.

"You all right? Millie Rae is fine. I talked to her. I did some digging into the recent sale of the club." Stan forced Reese to sit in the chair he'd just abandoned and sat between Reese and the door. "Turns out your friend Naomi is more vindictive than you first thought. She made the club more popular than her dad ever did. More because of the drugs she passed through there, but selling it was all her doing. A way to stick it to her old man. It seems like that way to me."

Reese leaned forward and put his elbows on his knees. His vision fogged as his brain tried to process all that Stan had told him.

"Naomi told me one time that her father wanted her to be a corporate worker. She said that he wouldn't trust a woman to do his job as well as he did," he said slowly.

"She wanted her father to turn in his grave because of what she was doing." Reese shook his head. "She tore it all down out of spite."

He shook his head and leaned back. Everything he'd learned about Naomi fit the bill of what Stan had found out.

Reese stared at Stan for a long moment. "What do I do?" he asked softly.

Stan looked at him with more sympathy than Reese deserved considering all he'd done to hurt Stan.

"My advice? You and Millie Rae get out of here. The guys I talked to at the precinct were very curious how you'd managed all you had in such a short time. They said they'd ask around if they could work a deal for you, but don't hold your breath. Millie Rae is not in as much danger. I don't know if she knew what was going on at Rouge Palace, but with the place shut down, it could be a new start for her. As for you, I bet Mitch is gunning to get rid of everyone associated with Naomi, regardless if you helped give him eyes on her operation. I can't say if he knows names and faces yet, but everything I've learned about the guy shows he's thorough."

Reese hung his head.

"I think he knows I'm staying here. I had another message besides yours and Millie Rae's. I didn't recognize the number."

His fear was paralyzing him. He felt as though Mitch could see into the room at this very moment.

"He probably has no problem taking me out along with the rest of the loose ends."

Stan stood and pulled Reese up by the shoulder.

"Let's get you out of here. How much cash do you have?" Stan's activity shook Reese from his stupor.

"Maybe a hundred on me."

Stan pushed Reese towards the door. They headed out of the hotel through the back entrance. Stan shoved Reese into the driver's side of his truck.

"You're going to stay at my office. Drive this. Give me the keys to your car. Do they know what you're driving?"

"I don't think so."

"I'll follow you in that." He took the keys that Reese handed to him.

"It's the small gray truck parked in the back corner."

Stan nodded and ran a hand through his hair.

"You'll be fine."

"Thank you, Stan."

Stan nodded before jogging around the corner towards the other truck as Reese turned the ignition.

Reese fully expected something dramatic to happen to Stan on the way back to his office. He'd waited with trepidation as Stan had started the little truck, fully expecting it to go up in flames. By the time Reese had parked Stan's truck in the office parking lot, he was a wreck of nerves. He hated that Stan had taken the man's truck, and he told him so by the time Stan pulled into the parking lot next to Reese.

"You should have let me drive that," Reese said, his voice coming out harsher than he'd ever heard it.

Stan closed the door and locked the cab before handing the keys back to Reese.

"I know how to spot a tail, and I wanted to see if anyone followed the truck." He got into his own truck and pulled out some papers from the backseat before gesturing at Reese to follow him. "I didn't see anyone following us from the hotel, so that's a good thing. I've been watching myself, and they haven't caught on to the fact that I'm helping you. You should be safe to stay here."

They rode the elevator up to Stan's office. It was just as Reese remembered it, but he was so stressed and anxious that strange details stood out to him. The stitching on the chairs, the half-full coffee cup that sat on Stan's desk. The smell of clove that he hadn't noticed the last time he'd been there, no doubt lingering from another client.

Stan sat him down in one of the chairs and set the folders on his desk. He puttered about, grabbing Reese a cup of tea and setting it down in front of him before pulling the blinds shut despite the dreary day. Reese took the cup of tea and held it in his hands, the warmth permeating his frozen fingers and softening his emotions. He took a deep breath and sipped at the drink before looking up at Stan as he finally came to sit in front of him.

"I made this entire mess," Reese said. He didn't want Stan's sympathy. He didn't need it. It would have felt like a wasted effort at this point. What he needed was an ally to help him get through the next few days alive.

"You sure dug yourself into a deep hole very quickly, Reese, but I can't blame you for trying to save your skin. Going to cops would have most likely gotten you killed, and I don't know if they would have believed you anyhow. They've been trying to infiltrate these organizations for years. I doubt Naomi would have let you decline her offer. She had you backed into a corner."

172

Stan pulled out one of the folders from the pile he'd brought in and handed it to Reese. Reese looked in the second folder and found himself looking at a picture of two young girls. He didn't recognize either of them, but they had their arms wrapped around each other, happy smiles on both girls. One was slightly taller, her round face framed by twin braids. The other girl seemed timid, her face slightly behind the other girl's. Her smile was more reserved, but he could see nothing but youthful joy in her face. He waited for Stan to explain.

"It was hard to find, but I think Naomi's uncle had a kid. He'd always dealt in drugs, but it blindsided him that his daughter was using. Messed her up real good. The girl died of an OD in high school. I guess the uncle stopped producing for a while, and that's when Naomi's dad stopped buying inventory from him. He falls off the radar for a while, but after Naomi gets thrown out of the family business several years later, she approaches him with some information. Turns out, Naomi's father knew all about his brother's kid being a drug addict. Didn't do anything to dissuade her from using because she brought in more customers. Naomi convinced her uncle the best way to get back at her father was to run his drug operation into the ground. They started up small, had Naomi get a corporate job like her daddy always wanted, but they started distributing on their own turf before moving into Mitch's."

Reese looked up as Stan sat back and took a drink of his coffee. He grimaced, only now noticing that it had been sitting there for some time and got up to make another cup.

"That's fine," Reese said as Stan moved around behind him. "But I don't understand what this has to do with my situation."

"You just have horrible luck," Stan said as he came to sit back down. He tapped the face of the smaller girl in the picture.

"By all accounts, that's Naomi. And the other girl is the one who OD'd. You thought you were just getting blackmailed into running drugs for Naomi because you were in the wrong place at the wrong time. You managed to work your way into a family drug war that has some serious comeuppance headed its way."

The coffee pot gurgled from the far side of the room.

"Naomi needed someone to help her expand into Mitch's territory by taking large amounts of product from her uncle's house to her dealers in the city, and she needed someone who couldn't say no." Stan shook his head. "I'd say you screwed yourself the day you started being soft on Millie Rae. If you hadn't been so frequent at the bar, this might have all passed over you. Now? You're in the middle of it, and it's about to implode. Neither Mitch nor Naomi have anywhere to go with the extra policing coming into the area because of all the rich people moving in. Implosion is their only option."

Chapter Fifteen

Stan left Reese to his thoughts as he moved about the office. Reese set the pictures down and held on to his cup of tea. Stan was right. Righter than he might ever know. Everything came back to Millie Rae. It all came back to that first night when Lester had taunted him by the garbage bins, and Reese had gone into Rouge Palace because he was sick and tired of people treating him like nothing. Millie Rae was his beginning, but he had no idea if he'd get an ending with her. Based on what he'd learned from Stan and what he'd seen of Mitch's retaliation against Naomi, his days were more likely to end with a bullet.

"I could run," he said, hoping Stan would have some way to help him disappear.

Reese looked over his shoulder to where Stan stood, reading a file he'd pulled from a drawer. Stan stared at Reese for a few moments before saying anything.

"Honestly, Reese, it's the only good chance you have. I've been doing P.I. work for a long time, and the only reason I put these pieces together was that you helped connect the dots for me."

He sat down next to Reese and took the cup from his hands. Reese had nothing to hang on to now but Stan's words.

"Convince Millie Rae to leave with you, if that's what it'll take you to leave. You don't come back here." He sighed and stood.

"I have a meeting across town. Stay here as long as you

want." Reese heard some rustling, and a lump of cash fell onto his lap. "Take that and get yourself out. My parting gift."

Reese stayed in Stan's office for some time after he left. He only moved from the chair to fill up his teacup. His hand ached, and he knew he should clean it again, but it seemed pointless. He left the blinds down, but he watched the clock tick by hour by hour as he tried to come up with a reason good enough to get Millie Rae to leave her grandmother's home. Getting fed up with waiting in Stan's office, Reese grabbed the keys to the small truck and headed out. He took the money that Stan had gifted him. He wanted to thank his friend for all that he'd done, but he had nothing to give, so he tidied up, took out the trash, and left.

Reese arrived at the diner ten minutes before he'd asked Millie Rae to meet him there. He had no way of knowing whether she would show, but he parked and went inside. The diner looked and smelled the same as the last time he'd been there, which Reese found immediately irritating and confusing. His whole world was falling apart, and there were people ordering coffee and dinner like nothing was happening. He sat down at a table and gripped the edge of the table for support. He considered sinking under the table to rot and gather dust like the abandoned French fries and straw wrappers. The waitress said nothing as she dropped off a glass of water and a menu. He touched neither, instead keeping his gaze focused outside, waiting for Millie Rae.

He had almost given up hope when he heard Millie Rae's voice from behind him. "You walked right past me," she said.

He turned to see her and grabbed onto her hand like a lifeline. She gave a startled exclamation as he pulled her onto the bench next to him.

"Millie Rae, you need to listen to me," Reese said, his hands frantically shaking in hers. "We're in trouble. This whole thing is my fault, yes, but you need to leave town with me."

Her mildly concerned face grew serious as she took in his haggard appearance. "I told you that I didn't have anything to do with Naomi's drug running."

"Please, just listen to me. Yes, I made a mistake, but I was trying to protect you from the mess I made. You have to understand that."

"And what security do I get that getting out of town and staying low will do anything? You've just told me to leave everything. Are you crazy?" She turned and quickly rattled off two orders to the waitress before turning around.

"You want me to forgive you? I can almost believe you that you got roped into Naomi's scheme without meaning to, but a lot of good people say that." She took a drink of water and looked around the diner. "I don't want to leave. This place is my home. Whether it's a drug dealer trying to push me out, or some new high-rise moving into the area filled with people thinking they're better than me, I won't be bought out. I'm not content running. That might be fine for you. I'm beginning to think this place might be safer without you in it."

She thanked the waitress as she came back with the food. Millie Rae said nothing as she ate. Reese pushed his food around his plate, anxiously waiting for her to finish. After she finished her food, she reached over and squeezed his hand.

"I think you know I'm right."

She got up out of the booth and nodded to him, a slight smile on her face before walking away.

He would do whatever Millie Rae asked of him. He'd known that from the beginning, and he couldn't let her down. She was his drug. And she was right. If she wouldn't run, he would find a way to make sure she could stay safe where she was. And he only had one option that he could see. He'd go to Mitch and plead his case.

He hadn't realized it was nearing midnight when he pulled up to Mitch's house. He saw the time as he scrambled from the cab, wondering how he'd lost track of time so easily. He hurried up to the house and knocked. He was empty-handed, but he was willing to do whatever it took to get Millie Rae her wish. Reese took an instinctive step back when the door opened. He saw the gun in Adam's hand. Reese raised his hands, noting without shame that they were shaking.

"I need to talk to Mitch, please."

Adam led Reese back to the same room he had seen Mitch in before. The hulking man nodded and left the room before either Mitch or Reese said anything. Mitch, to his credit, did not seem overly insulted considering the time. Reese would have tried to come in regardless, but having the man who had shot Naomi in a potentially decent mood was a boon he would take.

"I'm surprised to see you here," he said as he took in Reese's appearance. "Get into some sort of trouble with your hand?"

Reese glanced down at the bandage and rubbed his forearm.

"Mitch, I know you shot Naomi, and I'm here about her."

Mitch laughed, his mouth opening wider than Reese thought possible. It was a laugh that cooled his blood. It was high-pitched and sounded like a hyena. He hadn't denied that he'd shot Naomi. He probably felt that he didn't need to, considering Reese was in no position to report him for it.

Mitch shifted in his seat and groaned. "Look, if you have something to bargain with regarding Naomi, I'll listen, but you better hurry up about it."

He got up and started to move past Reese, no doubt to order

Adam to kick him out, but Reese grabbed his hand in a surprisingly firm grip. Mitch looked down at Reese's hand before slowly bringing his eyes back up to level with Reese.

"I probably don't have to tell you that I could cut that hand off."

"I'll give you Naomi," he said, keeping his firm grip on Mitch's arm.

Mitch jerked, pulling himself free, but what Reese thought was a sound bargaining chip didn't seem to faze Mitch. "And what would I want with her? She's gut shot."

"I saved her. Her uncle and I."

At this, Mitch stepped back a little and scratched his neck. "Her uncle, hmm? Naomi wasn't lying the other night when she came here. Said her uncle was cooking for her. She could have saved her own hide, not being a vindictive bitch, but we both know that'd never happen. Tell you what," Mitch pulled out the walkie-talkie and called for one of the guys to come in. "You convince that old coot to start dealing with me, and I'll look the other way about you saving Naomi's ass. I can take care of her later."

Reese heard the door open behind him, and Mitch waved the man inside.

"If you'll escort our esteemed backstabber out, I think he has some work to do for us."

"I want out. That's the only way I'll talk to her uncle."

Reese felt Adam move towards him from behind just as Mitch stepped towards him, his hand clenched.

"You're not really in a position to bargain."

Reese crossed his arms with a bravado that he didn't feel. "If you want her uncle's product that badly, you'll let me do it my way. I doubt he'd listen to anything you have to say, knowing

179

you shot his niece."

Mitch lunged forward, grabbing Reese by the front of his shirt and pulling him forward, so they stood a hair's breadth apart. Reese clenched his injured hand tightly, the pain giving him the energy to not drop his gaze.

Reese heard Adam moving behind him, no doubt waiting to do the rest of Mitch's dirty work.

Mitch pushed Reese away. Reese stumbled but caught himself on a chair. Mitch smoothed out his hair as he went to the seat behind the desk.

"OK," Mitch said. "You convince him to deal with us. Tell him we'll pay fifteen percent more than what Naomi was paying. Come back to me with the answer tomorrow night."

"What about Naomi?"

Mitch shrugged. "What about her? She'll die, and no one will care. Even if you did patch her up, that wound needs medical care."

Her uncle might care, Reese thought, remembering the way the man had patched her up.

Mitch eyed Reese for a moment before shrugging. "That old man lost any love he had the day his daughter died."

Reese pulled into the driveway of the farmhouse in the early morning hours. He kept his headlights turned off as he parked. He doubted the man would have anything kind to say if Reese woke both him and Naomi up at this time. He shut off the ignition and quietly closed the door. He didn't bother locking the car. It hadn't been locked when Reese had first received the keys, so he simply pocketed them and walked around to the front of the house. He pulled aside the screen door and tried the main door, the handle turning smoothly in his hand. He thanked rural

180

customs and quietly closed the doors behind him.

All the lights were off in the house, and he could hear the man snoring down the hall. Reese tiptoed to the bathroom and closed the door. He opened the bandage from his hand and inspected the wound. He hissed as the motion of pulling the gauze broke the scab forming on the cut. The color of the blood where it had dried on the gauze and around his hand was a dull, rusty brown, but the fresh blood was rich and bright. He threw the old bandage away in the trash bin and sought replacement pads underneath the sink. Before wrapping his hand back up, Reese looked at the meat of his hand, at what was inside him.

He wasn't pleased with what he found. He could see the muscle of his palm spasm as another wave of pain went through the area. The idea that all of this existed underneath his skin had the gorge rising in his throat. Disgusted, he quickly covered up his hand and put the things away. He didn't know if he would get an infection, maybe there was one already spreading through him, but he wouldn't know until he saw other symptoms appear.

He turned off the light and was creeping back towards the living room, intending to sleep on the couch until either Naomi or the man was awake when he heard Naomi calling him from her room.

He quickly went in, surprised she had the strength to call out to him, and turned on the light. She cursed and shielded her eyes. One hand still wrapped protectively around her abdomen, but it looked as though her uncle had helped her change clothes. She wore a gigantic shirt that made her childlike. Reese drew up next to her and took a moment to study her face. For Mitch's posturing that she would be dead soon, Reese thought she didn't look overly worse than she had when he'd seen her earlier. It spoke volumes that she was able to remain awake with her head propped up slightly.

"Do you want some water?" Reese asked quietly as he reached for the pad and paper he'd left there earlier. He moved to hand it to her, but she shook her head, both to the paper and the water.

"Had some earlier," she said, her voice a whisper scratch.

"Are you in pain?"

She glared at him before flipping her middle finger at him.

"Right. Sorry. Can I get you anything for it?" Reese asked, to which she shook her head.

He sat there and took stock of how she looked. The bags under her eyes had darkened, and the hollows of her cheeks were more apparent. He realized it was the first time he'd seen her with her hair down, and it didn't do her any favors. The way it clung, sweaty and dirty to her scalp and face, made her look like a skull with a wig attached. He kept these thoughts to himself and tried to hide his revulsion at the faint smell coming off her.

"I went to Mitch's," he said, unsure where to begin, and saw her eyes narrow in anger.

Chapter Sixteen

"Bastard," she croaked.

Even knowing that she couldn't hurt him, he held up his hands defensively.

"I went to see what he knew," he said, which was partially the truth. "He isn't concerned with you anymore."

She leaned against the pillow, her eyes closing in exhaustion as she mouthed what Reese could only assume was the same word she'd just used for him.

"He offered me a deal I couldn't refuse, Naomi." Reese clenched his bad fist, the pain bringing the situation to a critical point.

He saw her mouth move, but he had to lean closer to hear what she was saying.

"You sold me out."

Reese leaned back and shook his head. "I didn't. I told you Mitch doesn't care about you. But he said that if I can convince your uncle to provide the product to him, he'd leave Millie Rae and me alone."

She was fighting to get into a sitting position so that she could face him, but her wound wouldn't let her. He grabbed a pillow that had fallen to the floor to offer it to her, but she sank back down in the bed before he could get it behind her. He held it in front of him, as much for support as comfort.

"I need you to convince your uncle to take the deal," Reese said, not caring that he was pleading with the woman who had nearly destroyed his life.

She was thrashing her head back and forth, the motion throwing crazy shadows around the room.

He tried to quiet her because he could hear grumbling from the room where her uncle slept. Reese leaned over her and grabbed her by the shoulders. She gasped in frustration and pain, but she lay still again. Reese straightened the blankets around her before sitting down again. He picked the pillow back up and cradled it in his lap.

"You deserved to be caught," he said, his courage buoyed by the fact that she couldn't move from the bed.

"I won't give my product to anyone." She took several heaving gasps, her voice rising in volume, and Reese once again worried at her uncle waking up. "I hope you and your whore girlfriend get cut down by Mitch. It'll be the best you deserve."

Just for a moment, Reese pictured slamming the pillow down on Naomi's face. His hands shook as he took the pillow and set it down on the chair. Naomi hissed at him to stop as he walked out of the room, but he saw her smile when he returned. The smile turned to a frown when Reese set the man's dial-up on the chair and held the receiver to his ear.

"Yes, officer? I'd like to report suspicious activity and gunshots." Reese told the man the address and said that he would wait outside until help arrived.

Naomi thrashed in the bed.

"You fucking bastard." She lunged at him and gasped as the wound in her side made her slip off the bed. "I'll kill you. I'll destroy you." She knocked over the lamp on the bedside table. It crashed to the ground, and from the hallway, Reese saw the light to the man's room flick on.

Reese quickly backed out of the room and fled down the

hallway as Naomi screamed at her uncle to catch him. Reese should have expected the man would have a gun readily handy, but he didn't give it much thought until he heard the retort and felt a deep burning in his right thigh.

Reese toppled over, grabbing his leg, just as the old man fell on him. Fists fell all over Reese's face and hands as he tried to defend himself. The gun lay feet away, but Reese's only thought was to flee the madman on top of him. Reese caught the man in the chin and knocked him over. Reese scrambled up, his right leg threatening to collapse underneath him. He could feel the warmth of the blood seeping down the inside of his pants, and he tried to cover the wound with his hand as he limped outside towards the old man's truck.

He heard the man screaming inside, and he saw him appear at the front door just as he got into the cab and shut the door. Reese threw the truck in reverse and backed down the driveway as more shots fired and metal screamed as the bullets buried themselves into the truck's siding. Shaking in fear, Reese turned the truck around once he reached the road and threw it in drive. Reese reached down and tried to put a hand over the wound in his leg, groaning as the pain almost made him blackout. He drove the truck slowly down the road, sobbing as he heard the sirens approaching. He came to a stop and struggled to get out of the cab. He waved down the police cars as they approached. One stopped, the others speeding towards the house.

Reese's head felt cold, his eyes dimming as the officer tried to get information out of him. Reese was aware of mumbling his name and Stan's before sinking into unconsciousness.

Bright, sterile lights woke Reese. Everything around him was white and beige. Reese groaned as the pain resurfaced in his leg, accompanied by a splitting headache and a dry mouth. He turned his head to see monitors on all sides of him. He coughed and tried to reach for a water glass on the bedside table, but his arm stopped short by the handcuffs that held him to the bed. He stared at them for a moment before a moment in the corner of the room caught his eye. Millie Rae lay curled up on the couch near the window. He could see the deep bags underneath her eyes. Her hair was unkempt, her clothes wrinkled, and she seemed unaware that he had woken up.

He turned at a soft knock on the door to see Stan standing at the doorway with a drink in his hands.

Reese opened his mouth but only ended up producing a gravelly croak as his throat struggled to work. Stan quickly set his drink down on the bedside table and handed Reese the water. The handcuffs jingled as Reese took the glass, gulping the water down, stopping when he choked. Stan slapped him on the back, and Reese waved him off once he could breathe properly.

Stan pulled up a chair next to the bed and looked Reese over.

"I thought I said calling the cops wasn't the best of ideas."

Reese nodded, sipping the water slower this time.

"I know," Reese's voice was barely over a whisper. He touched his free hand to his throat.

"You've been out for eighteen hours," Stan said by way of explanation. "I guess you managed to spit out your name and mine before fainting on my buddy. You're lucky he was the one who stopped at your truck. He knew enough that he had the ambulance rush you here while he filled in the others with more details."

Reese jangled the handcuffs that kept him tied to the bed.

"Precautionary," Stan said, shrugging. "Since they don't know your association with the cartel, they aren't taking any

186

chances." Stan pointed to a cop standing just outside the door that Reese hadn't seen. "They called me because you mentioned my name. I've been able to fill in some of the details, but they were waiting for you to wake up so they could question you."

Reese hummed in his throat.

"Naomi and her uncle?"

Stan sighed and leaned back in his chair. "Naomi is currently being treated here, under much heavier surveillance than you are." Stan laughed at Reese's sour expression but glanced guiltily back at Millie Rae's sleeping figure.

"She's been here since I called her. Hasn't left your side. Said she's responsible for pushing you into this."

Stan ran a hand through his hair.

"Anyhow, Naomi's psycho uncle is in jail. They confirmed that he shot you, but he was ranting and raving about killing you, so they could have just brought him in and charged him on that. And the mountain of drugs he had stashed away in his barn."

Reese shifted his weight in the bed, gasping as the pain lanced down his right side. Stan stood up, reaching over Reese to push the nurse's call button.

"They said to call them as soon as you woke up, but I figured you'd want some questions answered before the circus descended on you."

Stan walked over to the door of Reese's room and opened it. He tapped the officer on the shoulder, who nodded, radioing into his shoulder com before coming to stand at the foot of Reese's bed. The commotion woke Millie Rae, who came suddenly awake as if she existed on a hair-trigger. Her eyes immediately went to his face, and she rushed to stand up just as the nurses came in, ushering everyone but them and the officer out of the room. Reese managed a small smile to her as she hovered outside the room's window before he turned and began answering the nurse's unending stream of questions.

Reese hardly got a moment of breath from when the nurses left and the cops began their string of questioning. The cop who sat down next to him was the same one that had been guarding the door. Stan had come back into the room after the nurses left and introduced the cop as Dan, one of the friends Stan had previously had on the force.

"Now, Reese," Stan said. "Dan does want to help you, but he's gonna do his job. I might suggest getting an attorney."

Dan glared at Stan but nodded. "You are allowed one. And given what Stan has told me of your situation, you shouldn't answer any questions without one present."

"What about Mitch?"

Dan nodded, pulling out a notepad. "If the information you provided us on Naomi and her organization is true, we will have more cause to pursue the person in question."

Reese nodded. He glanced out towards the nurse's station to see Millie Rae hovering just outside his room.

"Reese," Dan said, pulling his attention away from Millie Rae. "Are you refusing to talk without representation present?"

Reese saw Stan nodding emphatically behind the officer and hid his grin by drinking from his hospital cup.

"Yes."

Dan left after Reese promised to schedule a time to come down to the station for further questioning. Stan followed Dan out, leaving the door open. Reese pulled down the sheets and looked at how the doctor had wrapped his leg. It was an ever-present ache, and it wasn't until looking at his leg that he noticed they had treated his hand as well.

He looked up at a knock on the door and saw Millie Rae

standing in the doorway.

"The peanut gallery has left. You think it's safe to come back in?"

Reese smiled at her and nodded. She approached him slowly and sat down next to him in one of the stiff chairs she pulled from the side of the room.

"Aside from getting shot, how do you feel?"

She reached out and took his uninjured hand in his, tracing the lines on his palm.

"I'm not entirely sure," Reese said, his voice still feeling scratchy. "I guess I don't believe that the danger with Naomi is over. And that doesn't say anything about what Mitch might do to me if he finds me."

Millie Rae's fingers were still on his palm. She looked up at him, her eyes tracing over his face.

"I honestly don't know, Reese. Maybe the cops will have something to say about it. Maybe Mitch will just leave you alone?" She seemed to frown at her own words and shook her head. "But I imagine that's simply wishful thinking on my part."

Reese nodded, not saying anything in response. He stared out the window for a few moments before looking back at her.

"I can't stay here," Reese said, surprising himself. He pulled his hand away and clasped both in his lap. "I wanted to protect you from Naomi, and I guess I did that, but after everything that has gone on, I'm not sure I can live in this town."

Millie Rae nodded, not looking at him. He heard her suck in a breath, and she reached out to grab a tissue off the nightstand.

"I can't say I'm shocked," she said after a moment. Her voice sounded like she was talking around rocks, gravely and halting. She drew in another breath and looked back at Reese. Her eyes were wet, but her gaze was steady. "Maybe it was false hope that you would stay here with me. Despite our rough start together, I thought maybe we could have made something with each other."

Reese put his hand on top of hers and squeezed.

"I guess I thought that, too. And I think I wanted that for the longest time, but it is so hard to live in this area. Between the gangs and getting pushed out because I can't afford to live here.I don't really see another option." He gave her a sad smile. "Is it too much to hope that you would come with me? We could make a new start together?"

Despite the tiny sliver of hope that she might say yes, Millie Rae was already shaking her head.

"You know I can't. Or won't, I should say. I won't let anyone tell me where I can or cannot live. This is my town, and I plan to stay here." She sniffed again. "Do you know where you'll go?"

"No, but some peace and quiet doesn't sound bad after everything."

Reese remembered the house neighboring the Park's place.

"Maybe a place with a little bit of land. I've only really known the tiny apartment I had with my parents. I think something secluded and spacious like that might be good. Even if I end up living in a trailer, I think having space to call my own sounds nice."

Millie Rae stood and kissed his temple.

"Well, maybe once you're settled, I can come to visit?" She went to the sink in the room and tore off a piece of paper towel. On it, she wrote her address and tucked it on the table. "Don't be a stranger, and you'll always have a friend here."

"I won't be able to leave soon," Reese said, feeling her draw away. "I still have to talk to the police."

Millie Rae shook her head. "I don't want to know what goes on with that. Just let me know wherever you settle. We'll figure ourselves out from there."

Reese nodded, his heart heavy. "You need the dramatic exit?"

Millie Rae smiled down at him. "Only so you don't see me cry."

She turned away from him and gathered her things off the couch. She didn't look at him as she left, and Reese didn't say anything more to her as she closed the door behind her.

Chapter Seventeen

Several Months Later

Reese heard the car coming up the road before he saw it. A benefit of living out in the middle of nowhere was that people couldn't easily sneak up on him. He opened the door of his small R.V. and saw the silver flash of a truck as it broke through the trees. He could see Stan's profile in the driver's seat, and he waved. Reese walked out to meet him as Stan parked in the small gravel space that served as a turnaround. Stan got out of the truck and took a few moments to look Reese up and down.

"Looks like this place agrees with you, although you'd have a hard time telling you apart from the wilderness," Stan said as he held out his hand for Reese to shake.

Reese knew that he looked nothing like the pale, wan figure Stan had helped from the hospital weeks ago. Reese still walked with a limp, but spending time in the sun had done him wonders, and out here he didn't have to worry about someone calling the cops when he woke up yelling in the middle of the night because of nightmares. Reese's clothes still hung loose on him, but his skin was tanned from the time spent in the sun. He hadn't bothered to cut his hair since moving out to the trailer, so it hung down to his collar. It was still fine and pale, but since no one was around to comment, Reese hadn't bothered with its upkeep.

Stan moved back to the truck, took out several boxes from the back, and set them by the trailer's front door. Reese moved to help him, but Stan waved him off.

"I brought beer, mostly for me, but I got canned food, pasta and pasta sauce, and several gallons of water that should last you until I come back."

Stan moved into the trailer, and Reese followed. Stan set the boxes in the kitchen without preamble and began putting things in cupboards.

"How is Millie Rae?"

Stan paused for a moment to look over his shoulder at Reese before continuing his work.

"She's good. Last time I stopped by her place to drop off your last letter, she asked how you were doing. She wants to see you, Reese."

Reese toyed with the broken piece of vinyl coming off the trailer's table.

"Maybe once the trial is finished."

"Did I tell you what they're replacing Rouge Palace with?" Stan asked, moving away from the subject.

"It's supposed to be a building with shops on the bottom and apartments above it. I looked at the pricing, and it seems absurd. I might have to move out here with you one of these days."

Stan finished putting things away before grabbing a glass and pouring himself some water.

"Why don't you come back to town with me tonight? I know it's over a two-hour drive back, but you don't have to see anyone you don't want to. We can grab some takeout and hang out at my place."

Reese knew that Stan was talking about Millie Rae. He did want to see her. It was just that seeing her brought up memories of Naomi and everything that Reese had gone through to assure Millie Rae's safety.

"Reese, just breathe," Stan said, putting his water down and putting his hand on Reese's shoulder.

Reese focused on taking several deep breaths, aware that he had been teetering on the edge of a panic attack. Reese nodded to Stan and brushed his hand away.

"Thanks. I'm fine."

"What if I stayed out here with you?" Stan asked, picking up his water glass and coming to sit across from Reese. "I'm sure I have some cards in my truck. We could play poker and make some dinner?"

"That would be fine."

Reese found out that Stan was a pretty good cook. He surprised himself by eating two servings of the spaghetti that Stan made. Clearing the dishes, Stan brought in the pack of cards that he had in his truck. After a few hands, Reese sat back.

"I can't keep playing you. You're taking me to the cleaners."

Stan chuckled as he shuffled the deck.

"You won one hand."

Reese snorted.

Walking Stan out to his car later that evening, Reese paused, taking in the quiet nature of the area around him.

"I'm scared Mitch will find me if I show my face back in town again. Naomi is in jail, but she was only half of my problems."

Stan closed the door to his truck and leaned against the side of it. Reese couldn't read his expression in the dying light, but he trusted Stan.

"I get that, believe me, I do, but I think Mitch would be a fool to go after you right now. We're awaiting trial for Naomi's crimes, and you're a star witness, but you're not the only witness. I've been keeping in touch with my buddies on the force. Since the whole area has had such an influx of new residents, they've added a bunch of new cops to the roster. Yeah, there have been issues in your old neighborhood where the petty thievery and break-ins have gone up because people can't resist the money coming into the area, but these new kinds of people don't tolerate their law enforcement being lax at their job. Any complaint is being treated as important because the cops want to look good in the eyes of the people moving in. Mitch has to be laying low right now. I honestly wouldn't be surprised if he moved his operations to a different part of town where the cops are less keyed up on making a good impression."

Reese shook his head and stuffed his hands in his pockets.

"That may be, but coming into town still scares me."

He sighed and looked back at his trailer.

"Did you end up walking down to that convenience store I told you about? It's a couple miles, but you can always go there in a pinch if you need something."

Reese nodded.

"The people are nice there. I like it up here. I like the quiet. This place is small, but it's mine, and no one is trying to force me out just because they think I've overstayed my welcome."

Stan chuckled. "You got me there. The people coming in keep throwing their money around demanding better things, but I see many people who can't afford to live in the area now because of the rising prices. Whether the newcomers don't see it or refuse to see it, I'll never know."

"Do you know what Millie Rae is doing for work?"

Stan shook his head.

"I didn't ask the last time I spoke with her. I can find out.

Tell her you were asking. She'll probably tell me that you can ask her yourself when you visit."

Reese rolled his eyes and nodded.

"You're probably right. Well, thank you for coming out. Same time in two weeks?"

Stan nodded and got into his truck, waving out the window as he drove down the drive.

Reese was washing dishes when he heard a car coming up the road several days later. His hands froze in the soapy water before he quickly turned around and peeked between the blinds.

The vehicle was unfamiliar, and he couldn't see who was driving. His hand immediately flew to the knife he had just washed. Gripping it with a shaking hand, he waited until the car pulled to a stop in the gravel and the driver's door opened. His blood ran cold when Adam stepped out of the car.

The man had always looked intimidating when Reese had dealt with him in the past, but seeing him now made Reese feel beyond exposed and vulnerable. Reese didn't move from his position, knowing that any movement would probably alert Adam to his presence.

Reese heard Adam's footsteps grow louder as he walked up to the front of the trailer and banged on the door. The force reverberated through the trailer, and Reese could feel it through the floorboards.

"Reese, open the door. I'm not an idiot," Adam shouted from the doorstep.

Reese refused to move, his hand tightening on the knife in his hand.

"If you don't open this door, I'll force my way inside, and you won't like what I do to you if we don't keep this civil."

Reese watched Adam take a step back and cross his arms. Reese shuddered.

"How did you find me?" Reese called from inside the trailer.

"Open the door, Reese."

Reese reached his free hand down and turned the knob. He hadn't removed the security chain when the door crashed inward, hitting him square in the head, and everything went dark.

Reese felt a pounding in his head before he opened his eyes. Even through his eyelids, Reese groaned at the painful light that already seemed too bright. Carefully opening his eyes, he found himself sitting on a lawn chair outside of his trailer.

The bright sun made the pounding of his head even more acute, and he blinked several times to try and see clearly. He heard the crunch of steps in the gravel behind him, but he couldn't turn around as he found his wrists and ankles bound to the arms and legs of the chair. He turned his head, wincing against a fresh wave of pain in his head, and saw Adam coming around the side of the chair to stand before him.

Reese squinted up at him and shook his head at the warm trickle of blood he could feel sliding down his temple towards his jaw.

"You should have opened the door when I first knocked," Adam said. In his hands, he held the knife that Reese had been holding. Adam pulled up another folding chair and sat in front of Reese.

"So, Reese, it seems like life has been treating you decently since you decided to flip on Naomi."

Adam turned the knife in his hand as he leaned back in his chair.

Reese blinked, still frantically trying to clear his head.

197

"I had no choice."

His voice felt gravelly, like he'd somehow swallowed some of the grit that his chair now sat on. "She was going to kill me, or her uncle was. I haven't said anything about you or Mitch to anyone."

Adam chuckled. "Oh, don't worry. We have our own connections in the police force. We'd have known if you ratted on us."

"Still." He leaned forward in his chair and pressed the tip of the blade into the muscle of Reese's thigh. "We want to make sure it stays that way. See, I'd like to get rid of you and call it a day, but Mitch is convinced you're his 'lucky penny', as he calls it. He says that because you managed to fumble your way into taking out Naomi, our sales have gone through the roof."

Reese whimpered as the knifepoint pressed deeper into the fabric of his jeans, the point digging into flesh.

"I haven't said anything," Reese said again. He leaned as far back as his restraints allowed him to, desperate to get away from Adam and the blade.

"Stop it," Adam snapped, lifting the blade off Reese's thigh. "I said we know that. Mitch wanted me to pass along a message to you. See, because you've done us a good favor, we're going to do you a favor as well. We won't kill you, but we are going to leave you a little reminder that we're always one step away from finishing the job should you decide to say anything."

Adam leaned forward and untied Reese's hand that had the fresh scar from when he'd burned Naomi's car. Adam traced the jagged, white line with the knife tip before putting the blade next to the scar and began cutting deep.

Reese screamed as the blade cut through flesh and muscle and almost threw up when he felt it bump up against sinew and bone. Reese tried to yank his hand away, but Adam's grip was too strong, and any movements sent waves of pain up Reese's arm.

Once he'd finished, Adam dropped Reese's hand. It hung limply to his side, bleeding freely into the dirt. Reese's head fell forward onto his chest, but Adam's hand gripped his chin, forcing him to meet the other man's gaze.

"You know very well we'll do worse if you open your mouth. Mitch may think you're a lucky penny, but you're also a scared rat who is always looking out for himself." Adam patted Reese on the cheek and dropped the bloody knife into Reese's lap.

"I'm sure you can free yourself." Adam stood up and tapped the corner of his eye. "Be seeing you around."

Reese sobbed as Adam made his way back to the car and backed down the driveway. Reese began thrashing as soon as Adam was out of range, desperate to escape the restraints he found himself in. He knocked the knife onto the ground and nearly toppled the chair over in the process before he was able to slow his breathing and think logically.

Fighting against the pain, he used his wounded hand and barely managed to grasp the knife. He had no idea how long it took him to cut himself free, but once he'd managed to cut himself loose from his restraints, he was exhausted and dripping in sweat.

Cradling his arm, he stumbled towards the trailer and into the bathroom, where he dug around for any type of antiseptic. He found a small emergency kit behind the mirror and opened the bottle of hydrogen peroxide with his teeth. He nearly fainted when he poured the liquid over the wound, the sink turning pink with his blood. Ripping open the several packs of gauze that he found, Reese carefully placed them on the wound, trying not to panic when the blood quickly seeped through the fabric. He grabbed a hand towel and wrapped that around the gauze, holding it in place. The pain had turned into a hot throbbing that carried up his arm, but he was able to clean the wound on his head. It had already started to clot, so he wiped the dried blood off his face and went into the kitchen.

He pulled open a drawer and dug past the pens and pencils to pull out a cell phone. Stan had given it to him so that he could periodically check in on Reese. Reese didn't usually bother calling Stan because he knew his friend was busy, but he dialed his number and sat down on the trailer sofa while it rang.

Chapter Eighteen

Stan made it out to the trailer in record time. Reese was still sitting on the couch when he heard the car pull up. He'd dozed a bit waiting for Stan, so Reese felt a wave of panic before he glanced out and saw the familiar truck. Stan hurried to the trailer and cursed when he saw the damage to the front door. He quickly took in Reese's state and helped him stand.

"We're going to have to take you into town," Stan said as he helped Reese down the stairs of the trailer. "What, or rather who, did this to you?"

Reese shook his head as he made his way to the truck and buckled himself into the passenger seat. Stan glared at him for a minute before slamming the door shut and heading around the front of the car to get in the driver's seat. He started the car, and they headed down the bumpy dirt road away from the trailer. Each bump fired pain through Reese's hand and arm, but he gritted his teeth and looked away from Stan.

"I'm not an idiot, Reese. I can think of one other person who might find it in their best interest to threaten you," Stan said as they turned onto the county road towards the highway.

"It was just an accident," Reese said, watching the fields pass by.

He heard Stan's sigh, but neither said anything for the rest of the drive back towards town.

Reese was thankful that Stan didn't take him to the emergency room. Instead, they went to a local urgent care on the north side of town. Reese told the nurse that he'd cut it when he was cooking food. He didn't know that she fully believed him, but she didn't say anything else as she numbed the area and gave him his stitches. She told him that he would have to seek help to regain complete muscle control of the hand since it had hit more than flesh, but Reese knew he would just have to make do with however it healed. Stan said nothing as they signed the forms for the care before leaving. They put his arm in a sling to keep it elevated and reduce movement of the arm as a whole.

Reese didn't fully expect Stan to drive him directly back to the trailer, and he didn't protest when Stan pulled up in front of his own house and turned the truck off.

Reese had stayed here for several weeks after his release from the hospital, so after Stan opened the front door, Reese went back to the guest bedroom that he'd stayed in and sat on the bed. The pain in his hand was slowly returning as the numbing wore off. He was considering dosing, partially because his body was exhausted from its ordeal, but also it would be a way to avoid any questions from Stan. As if he'd been summoned, Stan appeared in the doorway to the bedroom and leaned against the frame.

"You all right here if I go back to work?"

Reese nodded. "Thank you for coming and getting me and for taking me to the hospital."

Stan nodded, watching Reese from the doorway. Reese could see that Stan wanted to say something.

"Just say whatever it is you have to say," Reese said. He ran his good hand over his face and looked at Stan.

"I hate to see you've isolated yourself after everything you've done," Stan said. "Both the good and the bad, there are people who still want you in their lives."

"Millie Rae, you mean." Reese sighed and looked up at the ceiling to avoid Stan's eye contact.

"Just talk to her. I get that everything that happened to you happened because of her, but it wasn't her fault."

Reese refused to look at Stan, and eventually, Reese heard Stan's footsteps head down the hallway.

Reese knew that Stan was right. Reese knew that he was a coward, but every time he thought about Millie Rae, he couldn't help the overwhelming feeling of fear and dread that accompanied those thoughts. It had never been Millie Rae's fault, but now that Naomi was behind bars, the person most closely associated with all the events was Millie Rae. There was no way he could see her and not think about everything that had happened to him. Perhaps he could have found comfort in knowing he didn't have to explain himself, but it simply wasn't the case.

Reese leaned back in the bed and tried to make his hand as comfortable as possible. The pain was wearing him out, and he found his eyes drifting closed before he could pull the blanket over himself.

Reese woke to a banging sound. He sat up, forgetting where he was and jerked his hand. Pain raced up his hand into his arm, and he doubled over momentarily as he remembered why he was at Stan's house and not his trailer. He listened from his backroom as the banging, which turned out to be someone knocking on the door, stopped. Reese adjusted himself on the mattress, content to let whoever was at the door simply think no one was home, but when the knocking came again, he had to wonder if someone knew he was here.

He quietly walked down the hallway and made out a faint

silhouette of a person on the other side of the glass front door. Reese hesitated in the hallway, waiting to see if the person was willing to knock a third time, when the muffled voice of Millie Rae came from the other side of the door.

"Reese, Stan told me you were here. Now, you can get mad at him and hide from me, or you can grow a backbone and open up this door so we can talk."

Chapter Nineteen

Reese opened the door and almost immediately felt anxiety crawling its way up his spine at the sight of Millie Rae in front of him. She looked just about the same as he remembered, albeit more rested than the last time he had seen her at the hospital. She wore a pair of skin-tight jeans and a flowing, one-shoulder top. Her hair was braided, accents of gold glittering in the sunlight behind her. She looked a bit plumper than the last time he had seen her, and Reese fiddled with the hem of his threadbare shirt as he stepped back and allowed her inside.

He quickly shut the door behind her and locked it. Turning, he saw her taking stock of Stan's house, her back to him. Reese didn't say anything, content to let the silence fill the space between them, and he found that not staring directly into her eyes caused him far less anxiety, although it did still crawl along his shoulders.

"Listen," she said, still not turning towards him. "I know that you haven't wanted to see me. I get that. But there are some things that I want to say to you in person, so you just have to listen to me, and then I'll be gone."

Reese could see the tension in her back and felt his fade slightly. He stepped around to face her and motioned for her to take a seat on the couch.

She took a seat, and Reese sat down across from her in a chair. Millie Rae fidgeted with her hair for a few moments before sighing and looking at him.

"I know you were scared of everything that happened to you. Lord knows, I understand why you moved away from town, but I needed you. I needed someone to talk to about everything that had happened. Everything that happened to the both of us, and you wouldn't answer any of my phone calls." Her voice shook a bit, but she cleared her throat and shook her head. "Can't you understand that?"

Reese was silent for a few moments as he mentally adjusted to the fact that Millie Rae might have needed him more than he thought.

"I guess I hadn't thought that you would need to talk to me. To anyone, for that matter. You always come off as so self-assured that I had no doubt that you would bounce back and move on."

He shook his head, realizing how wrong he'd been for thinking that Millie Rae might not need someone to confide in.

"It's just that seeing you, being near you, brings up all these emotions." Reese cut himself off when he felt his voice begin to tremble.

Millie Rae nodded. "I know. I'm sorry." She paused for a moment before continuing.

"Can I ask what happened to your hand? Stan said not to be shocked when I saw you." There were frown lines between her eyebrows. "I'm sure it's painful."

Reese looked down to the sling and nodded. He debated whether or not to tell her the truth. "I don't want to talk about it right now."

He heard a soft affirmation come from Millie Rae, still unwilling to meet her gaze. They sat in silence for a few moments before Reese managed to work around the knot in his throat and speak.

"You look well. What kind of a job did you find after Rouge Palace shut down?"

"I started doing dance lessons out of my house," she said, a smile on her face. "Turns out, all that new money coming into town meant a lot of new kids needing a place to get away from their hard-working parents.

"It's good," she said, almost sounding surprised by herself. "I like it. I never thought I'd be the teaching type, but the kids don't look at you with judgment, not that I'd tell them where I previously worked. I've been thinking about renting out a small studio, but I haven't built up the courage to drop that kind of cash yet." She stared at him, her gaze soft. "It was a blessing that Rouge Palace shut down. I was killing myself there trying to save girls who didn't all the time want to be saved."

She took a breath and stood, walking over to where he sat and knelt in front of him. She put her hands on his knees when he tried to pull away from her.

"You did so much trying to help me, Reese. You did what you promised and fixed your mess with Naomi. Hell, the police would probably argue that you did more than just fix your mess. You solved a big problem for them."

Reese stared down at her. She was still Millie Rae. Still the woman who drawn him in that first night at Rouge Palace.

"I just don't see you the same way anymore," he said quietly.

Millie Rae nodded.

"That's okay. I can't say I'm shocked. But I can still be your friend and want you to be happy with your life without you constantly waiting for the other shoe to drop. So, here is my thought: you'll always have an open-door policy with me. Call me day or night. Do you still have your phone at the trailer? I'll call on the first Saturday of each month. If you answer and want to talk, great, but don't feel obligated."

She stepped up to him and put her hand on his face. Reese managed a small smile for her.

"I just want to be happy," he said, leaning his face into her hand.

Reese returned to the trailer the next day, packed full of things he would need for the next two weeks by himself. As they bumped up the drive, Reese glanced over to Stan, who hadn't said much about Millie Rae's visit the day before.

"I did talk to her, you know."

Stan nodded.

"I thought as much. Listen, Reese, I know it wasn't right of me to call her like I did, but—" Stan blew out a breath, letting the rest of whatever he was going to say hang between them.

"It's okay," Reese said, shifting in his seat. "I know why you did it. And I think I realized something talking to her." He took a breath before continuing. "I put her in a dangerous spot when I ran across Naomi that night. I put myself in a dangerous spot, too, but it didn't matter so much that I could get hurt. I didn't want Millie Rae to suffer because of my mistakes. I put her first, and I'd do it again, but it made me realize that I've never really put myself first. Working at the garage, I always bent over backward to make everything better for everyone else, even if it meant I suffered for it. I don't want to be that way anymore. I want to focus on myself. On a goal that makes me happy for me."

He glanced over to Stan as he pulled the truck up next to the trailer.

"Does that make me selfish?"

Stan cut the engine and turned to look at Reese.

"No, in fact, I think that makes you human. And I can't think of anyone else who could fault you for thinking the way you do."

Stan opened the driver's door and climbed out. Reese climbed out as well and dug in his pocket for the key to the front door. He looked to where the door had splintered by the security chain when Adam had burst inside. The key stuck in the lock because the door didn't quite sit on the hinges correctly, but Reese finally forced it open with his good arm and stood looking around.

In reality, it wasn't much nicer than the meager apartment he had lived in for most of his life, but in contrast, everything here was something he had either picked out or didn't immediately remind him of his parents. It was his place. Granted, it needed tidying after Adam had broken in, but he didn't feel violated like he thought he might upon seeing the place where he'd been attacked.

He heard Stan coming up behind him and moved farther into the trailer to give him space. Stan set several bags of dry goods on the table before taking a moment to look at the door.

"I think it should be fine. The hinges are a little bent, but otherwise, the door should still lock without an issue. It'll just stick a bit."

Stan and Reese pulled the rest of the bags into the trailer and put things away before Stan got in his car to head back to town.

Stan rolled down the window and looked at Reese before he drove away.

"I think you should give yourself a little credit, Reese. You're handling a crazy situation the best you know how. People aren't going to ask more from you than that. At least, not the people who actually matter."

He pulled the truck away and waved out the open window before disappearing around the bend of the drive.

Chapter Twenty

Reese cursed when he heard the phone ringing inside the trailer. Setting down the wood he'd carried to the woodpile, he wiped his hands on his pants as he hurried towards the sound.

He reached the phone on the third ring. Panting, he brought the receiver to his ear.

"Hello?"

"Reese." Millie Rae's voice came from the other end of the line. "It's good to hear your voice. I'm glad you picked up this time. It's been a couple weeks since I saw you, and I wasn't sure if you'd ever pick up."

Reese grabbed the water glass on the counter and took a drink before answering.

"Ah, yes. How are you doing?"

He could hear rustling coming from the other end of the line. Voices murmured in the background. He sat down at the kitchen table and took another drink of water.

"I'm good," came her reply. "I just finished up a class. I've actually got more students than I know how to handle at the moment. Makes me wonder if I shouldn't have done this years ago."

"I remember you saying that you didn't want to teach when you were younger."

Millie Rae mumbled something to someone in the room with her before replying to him.

"You remember me saying that? Well, I was probably right

to wait, but it surprises me how much I like what I'm doing now."

"I'm glad that you're doing well," Reese said. He leaned back in the seat and stared up at the ceiling, waiting to see if she would say more.

"Are you doing well, Reese?"

He could hear the hesitancy in her voice.

"Well enough," he said. He sought a lengthier explanation, but none came to mind.

"That's good to hear. What are you doing to keep yourself busy out there?"

"I've been trying to fix up the trailer. It wasn't in the best shape when Stan and I found it, so that's been keeping me occupied. It's hard work."

He glanced towards the bedroom, where he'd recently installed new wallpaper to the walls and fixed the broken doors on the storage hutch.

"You said you wanted to be happy. Does doing that make you happy?"

Reese raised his shoulders in a shrug, his eyes glancing over the rest of the trailer to places he had yet to repair.

"It keeps me busy. Look, Millie Rae, I need to go, but it was good to hear your voice." He heard her quick goodbye as he set the phone down in its cradle.

Leaning his head on his arm, Reese took several deep breaths before standing up and heading back outside. The fresh air cooled the sweat that had beaded up on the back of his neck. His hands felt clammy as he went back to stacking the wood at the woodpile.

"Am I happy?" he muttered to himself as he continued to work. "How would I know about being happy? All I know is that I feel calm. Happiness is a long way away for me."

Reese shuddered, knocked off-kilter by his own words. He straightened from his work and surveyed the area around him. The silence of the surrounding woods absorbed his guilt when he woke up screaming and sweating from the nightmares he had. The trail to the back of the trailer gave him peace when he walked it at night because he couldn't sleep.

The repairs to the trailer gave him flickers of pride as he made the place into somewhere he could stay long term.

But happy?

He pushed the question away as he returned to his work, content to let his mind fog over.

He worked until the sun began to set. Heading inside, he opened the pantry and took out some pasta and sauce that Stan had brought him the week prior. Pulling out two pots, he filled one with water and the other with the sauce.

Taking stock of what he had left, Reese frowned and counted the number of cans in the pantry. He counted a second time before reaching for the phone and dialing Stan's number.

"Hey, you're still planning on coming up at the end of the month, right?"

"Yep. You running low on supplies?"

Reese pushed aside several cans and recounted his food stores.

"Yeah, but I can go to the convenience store down the way and pick up stuff. I was just calling to see how things are going with the case."

Reese heard Stan let out a breath while Reese held his own.

"It's been going. I can't say that it's good or bad simply because there is a lot for the attorneys to go through. Naomi has buckled down and found a good lawyer. He's making things difficult. I think there's enough incriminating evidence that it'll be hard for even him to weasel her out of being sentenced."

Reese let out his breath and reached over to turn off the burner. He poured the pasta into a strainer and let it sit while he dug around for a bowl.

"That's good to hear. I, uh, talked to Millie Rae."

"Good for you. Did she say anything about wanting to see you next time you were in town?"

"I'm not really sure about seeing her next time."

"No problem. And remember, you have your last witness testimony next month. Get this under your belt, and you should be set."

Reese's hand tightened on the phone.

"I remember. Is there some way I don't have to face her?"

"You'll have people with you the whole time, Reese. Remember that. You're safe."

Reese thanked Stan again and hung up.

He salted and peppered the pasta before tossing it in a bowl and sitting down at the table. Reese picked at his food, his mind thinking about the court date less than a month away. He rubbed his thumb along the knotted scar on his palm.

It would be the last time he had to go back to the city. He took a deep breath as he felt his heart pick up pace at the thought.

Reese woke to his own screaming that night. He sat up, throat raw, covered in sweat. Fumbling for the light, he flicked it on, thankful for the generator outside. Putting his face in his hands, he tried to calm his breathing. He ran his hand through his damp hair, grimacing at the sticky feeling. Throwing the covers off, Reese slipped on a pair of shoes and went outside.

The dream wasn't always the same. This time, Reese ran from Naomi and her uncle only to find himself face to face with

Mitch. Mitch always wore a cruel smile on his face before the retort of the gun behind him sank bullets into his leg and chest.

The cool night air dried his clammy hands and hair, and he lifted his shirt off, the material soaked through. Sighing, he tossed the shirt back towards the open door of the trailer and pulled it shut.

He didn't bother with a flashlight on his walk. The moon and stars were enough that he could see that trail without any difficulty. It had amazed him when he first moved out here how bright the sky could be. He heard cracking in the brush beside him, some animal startled by his presence, but the noise didn't bother Reese.

By the time he finished the loop of the trail and returned to his trailer, his hands were only slightly shaky. His limbs felt heavy, and his mind was comfortably blank. He picked up his shirt when he opened the trailer. Going inside, he crawled back into bed and fell into a fitful sleep that lasted until morning.

Reese walked down to the convenience store the next morning with an empty backpack. He'd made the mistake the first time of carrying his groceries back in the plastic bags provided, and by the time he'd gotten back to the trailer, his hands were sore from where the plastic had pinched.

The convenience store was nothing special. It looked as old as the cracked cement road that it sat along. The paint had long peeled off, and the windows were covered in a layer of dirt that no one seemed inclined to clean off.

Reese walked past several people filling up their cars. Reese had learned that people around here generally stayed out of each other's business. The bell above the door dinged when he opened it, and the air conditioning felt good against the sweat he'd built up on his walk.

The man behind the counter grunted at him as Reese headed down the narrow aisles to the small selection of canned foods near the back. The selection never changed, so Reese filled his backpack with canned pasta sauce, beans, and a few cans of tuna fish before walking to the counter.

He pulled the stuff out of his bag, letting the man scan the items. He handed the man cash and put all the cans back in his backpack before zipping it up and taking his change. Reese was turning to go when the man spoke.

"You walk here every time you come, son?"

Reese froze, knowing that most people around here traveled by car. Singled out, Reese turned around and nodded, his hand tightening on the backpack strap.

The old man scratched his chin as he studied Reese.

"Your business is your own, but there ain't much around here to walk to, so you must be coming a ways. If you're interested, I got an old bike that needs a bit of work. I'd sell it to you at a discount. Might shave some time off your commute every time you come in for supplies."

Reese swallowed, nodding his head a fraction of an inch.

"I'll think about it."

The man nodded.

"Let me know next time you stop in what you think. It's around back if you want to take a look at it before you go."

The man pulled out a newspaper and began reading, signaling the end of the conversation.

Reese adjusted the backpack and left, hesitating before walking around back and looking for the bike the man had talked about.

What Reese found was a beat-up motorbike that had seen

better days. The fenders were rusted, and the weather had faded the lettering on it, so Reese couldn't tell what brand it was. The seat was cracked, and Reese could see old horsehair sticking out from underneath. A rusted metal storage frame sat behind the seat, and Reese pulled his backpack off and set it on the frame to test its size. With some bungee cords, it would hold a fair amount. Reese knelt down and poked at the tires, both flat, but the rims were in decent shape.

Putting his backpack on, Reese walked back around the store and back inside. The old man was still at the counter and looked up when he came in.

"How much would you ask for it?"

"I bought in '69 for three fifty. Figured with how much work it's gonna need, I'd let it go for one fifty."

Reese thought about it for a moment. His hands shifted on the straps of his backpack.

"I run a shop down the road that repairs vehicles since everyone around here likes to drive their trucks until they're turning into dust. If you know what you're doing, you can use the garage to fix it up."

"I'll take it, but I don't have the cash on me."

The man shrugged. "It hasn't gone anywhere in about twenty years. It'll be there when you have the cash. What's your name?"

Reese swallowed. The man had said more to him in the last half hour than he'd said to him in the last few months.

"Reese," he said cautiously. "Why are you offering me the bike now?"

The man pushed his baseball cap up his forehead and squinted at Reese.

"Had to know if you were sticking around long enough to offer it. We get a lot of drifters that only stay around a week or so, then move on. Seems to me like you're sticking it out in the area for a bit, and it's obvious that your feet are the only transportation you got." The man shrugged. "Seemed like you might find a use for it."

Reese nodded. He shifted his weight, his feet already tired from the walk down to the store. The man was right. Walking down to get food at least two times a week was wearing on his body. His shoes hadn't been made to withstand that amount of walking, and he'd found a hole in the sole of his left shoe last week.

"I appreciate it. Thank you."

The man waved him off. "You'll get it off my hands. Name's Mart, by the way. I'll see you around, Reese."

By the time Reese arrived back at the trailer, he knew he'd made the right decision to take a look at the bike. He set the backpack on the counter and sat down, his feet throbbing. He toed off his shoes and leaned back in the seat.

Despite his sweaty back and the pain in his feet, Reese felt a smile emerge. If he had a bike, he could explore the area. Look for a job that didn't require him to go back to the city. Despite living in the city his whole life, he was finding that his cabin felt more and more like a place he could call his own.

Chapter Twenty-One

Reese straightened his tie and glanced over at Stan, who sat in the waiting room with him. The trial was being held in the room next door. Reese could hear muffled voices as the case went on against Naomi.

Reese had requested to wait in a separate room until he was called to the stand. The less time he had to be near Naomi, see her face, watch her movements, the less time he had to fight down the panic that threatened to crawl up his throat.

Stan was providing his own witness statement today, but he looked calm as he sat next to Reese, sipping a glass of water that had been provided. Stan's suit was a charcoal gray.

"How many times do you get called to testify because of cases you've helped with?"

Stan glanced over to him before shrugging.

"It happens here and there. I usually just need to provide evidence. Photos, voice recordings, things like that. But with this case being what it is, they wanted me to come in and give a more detailed account of everything. Mostly what I communicated to the police."

Reese nodded and glanced down at his hands. He clutched the paper where he'd written down his statement. He didn't feel comfortable trying to come up with something on the spot.

"I just don't understand why I have to face her when I told the cops everything I know."

Reese heard Stan stand and move around before a water

glass appeared in front of him. Reese took it and held it.

"It helps to drink water. Going in dehydrated won't make you feel any better."

Reese glanced up to Stan, who sat back down. Reese sipped the water and set the cup shakily down on the table.

"Do you think they'll cross examine me?"

Stan shrugged.

"I honestly have no idea what Naomi's lawyer is trying to accomplish. There's so much evidence stacked against her that I think he's just trying to get her sentence down. If he does, you can always ask the judge if you have to answer a question, say you don't know if you really don't know the answer, and always tell the truth."

Stan rubbed his hand on the back of his neck and checked the time on his watch.

"Things are also going late, so they might not have time."

Reese meant to ask more, but a knock came on the door, and the bailiff opened it. He gestured to Reese with an impatient gesture of his hand.

Reese swallowed, sweat pricking underneath his armpits and down his back. He stood, anxiously smoothing his pants before clutching his testimony and moving towards the door. Stan said something behind him, but Reese didn't hear it as his senses zeroed in on giving him the strength to face the woman in the next room.

The room felt heavy as he walked inside. It was mostly silent, the people watching murmuring to themselves as he walked in. He tried to avoid eye contact with the defendant's table where he knew Naomi sat, and he managed it until he climbed up to the seat next to the judge and was sworn in under oath.

He sat down, his eyes going immediately to the orange jumpsuit that stood out garishly against the muted colors of the suits that everyone else wore. Her eyes bored into him. She looked thinner than when he'd last seen her. More feral. As if her time in prison had brought out even more of her heartless nature. Her fingers drummed against the table as she stared at him, a slight smirk thinning her lips.

Reese felt his breath catch in his throat, and he forced himself to look at the judge, who was saying his name. The woman was staring at him, and he stared at her for a moment before asking her to repeat the question.

"Would you please read your testimony to the court?" she asked.

She nodded to him in what Reese hoped was an encouraging gesture. She kept her gaze on him as he cleared his throat and leaned into the mike.

He began his testimony, his voice shaking, but as he read, he felt stronger, more sure of himself. He refused to look at Naomi's face, keeping his eyes on the paper as he read. In the back of his mind, he briefly wondered what effect his testimony was having on the trial, but he refused to look up until he finished reading.

When he had, Reese took a deep breath and glanced back to the judge, who nodded to him again. He looked over the prosecution table, wondering if they would stand and question him when movement to his right suddenly drew his gaze.

Naomi had stood, her body leaned forward as if she meant to throw herself across the courtroom at him. Her lawyer was quickly trying to get her to sit down, and the bailiff was immediately on guard.

"You're a worm," she snarled at him, even as the judge snapped at her to sit down.

Naomi ignored the judge, and Reese pulled back into his seat, desperate to keep as much distance between her and himself. She yanked against the chains that bound her feet and hands together.

"I should have shot you that first night I found you in the alley." She shook off her lawyer, who was telling her very firmly to stop speaking. "I should have gutted you and that whore you were so desperate to protect."

Naomi's lawyer finally managed to jerk her back into her seat, but she continued to spit threats towards Reese.

Reese felt trapped on the witness stand. He sunk further down into the chair and held his papers up in front of him as if they would shield him. The whole court was talking over itself at the treats Naomi had just made.

The judge banged her gavel, finally quieting everyone.

"Bailiff, take the accused back to the holding cell until she has had time to control herself."

Reese had no idea how the judge managed to keep her voice steady as she said this, but he watched as Naomi was yanked from her chair and escorted to a door and through it.

Both sides of lawyers requested to come up to the bench, but the judge waved them off.

"We'll wait until the bailiff has returned and escorted our witness out. I think he's faced enough onslaught today."

Reese nodded to her in thanks, unwilling to trust his own voice. The bailiff returned, taking Reese back to the waiting room where Stan waited.

Stan stood, seeing the expression on Reese's face. He rushed forward and gripped Reese by the shoulder as Reese sunk into a chair.

"What happened?" Stan asked as the bailiff returned through

the doorway, closing it behind him. "All of a sudden I heard all this noise from the other side of the room, but I couldn't tell what anyone was saying."

Reese shook his head, laying his head on his forearm. He took several deep breaths, willing his shaking to subside.

"I just want to go home," Reese said weakly. He raised his head and glanced to Stan, who was still sitting next to him. "I gave my statement, but then Naomi threatened me. She said she should have killed me that first night."

Reese reached over and gulped down his leftover water. Stan patted his arm and leaned back in his chair.

"If you riled her up enough that she said that in court, her chances of having any time dropped on her sentence just went to practically nothing. She threatened a witness in front of a judge." Stan shook his head. "You may have just intended to go in there and provide your testimony, but it sounds like you might have cut Naomi off at the knees."

Reese nodded, still shaking. Stan sat by Reese until the bailiff returned and gestured for Stan to follow him.

Reese said nothing as Stan passed him, knowing that Stan didn't need the type of reassurances that Reese had needed. Reese crossed his arms on the table and leaned his head on them, content to sit in the quiet until this nightmare was over.

Chapter Twenty-Two

The bailiff knocked on the door several hours later. Reese and Stan looked up. Stan had nearly paced a track in the carpet since he'd returned from his testimony.

"They're reading the verdict now." The man glanced between them. "You're welcome to come sit in the back while it's read."

Stan nodded, and he glanced to Reese. Reese toyed with the pen on the table, unable to look at the bailiff.

"It's the last time you'll ever have to face her," Stan said, his voice a comforting whisper. "Coming in shows her that you're not scared of her."

Reese blew out his breath and nodded. He stood, dropping the pen, and straightened his tie. He nodded to the bailiff, who escorted them down another hallway and to the back of the courtroom, where they stood, unable to find seating.

Reese could barely see the back of Naomi's head and, seeing the courtroom from this perspective, it seemed impossible that he had sat up there and given his testimony.

The jury came back in, and Reese felt his back tense as the verdict of guilty was given for every charge. No chance of parole.

Reese's body shook as Stan slapped him on the back and shook him. Naomi stood and was escorted out of the court, and Reese watched as she hobbled away, suddenly small and insignificant.

He turned to Stan and grinned, his mouth wide as a laugh as

relief flooded out of him. There was a sudden push towards the doors as people left the courtroom, and Stan and Reese moved with the current out to the front steps of the courthouse.

They skirted around the camera crews and newspaper reporters, who moved in on the legal team as soon as they were in view.

Reese watched the interviews from a step some distance away. He took a deep breath, savoring the moment again. The warm heat of the day made him loosen his tie and roll up his sleeves, but he was content to stand for a moment in the brightness.

"How does it feel?" Stan asked, standing next to him.

"Great," Reese said. "Just great."

"You wanna go grab a drink?"

Reese nodded, the mob of people at the front of the courthouse not looking like they were going anywhere anytime soon. Reese glanced over to Stan.

"Got anywhere in mind?"

"I was thinking we grab a six pack and head back up to the trailer." Stan started towards his truck, Reese matching his step. "After all this noise and fanfare, the quiet of the trailer sounds real nice." They got into the truck. "You might be on to something about living away from people. I swear, every time I go out there, I feel better. Too bad living out there would be bad for my business."

They stopped at Stan's house so he could change before picking up beer and making the long drive back to the trailer. It was dusk by the time they arrived, but still enough light to sit outside and drink a few beers before the sun completely disappeared.

Reese held the beer in his hand, a silly smile on his face. It kept appearing when he least expected it, and he took a drink, leaning back in his lawn chair. Stan sat across from him, staring out at the scenery.

"Have you thought any more about what you'll do now that you are having to look over your shoulder all the time?"

"A guy down at the convenience store is going to sell me his road bike. It gives me some mobility, but I might see what kind of work I can find up here. I've lived my whole life in a few square blocks. Now that I'm up here, I feel like I have freedom that I didn't before." Reese took another drink of his beer. "Maybe the city will feel different now that Naomi isn't a threat, but who knows. It'll take me a while before I'm ready to come into town regularly."

Stan nodded. He played with the beer in his hand before finishing it and crushing the can.

"Well, don't be a stranger." He stood, and Reese glanced up at him. "I'd stay, but I told myself I'd only have one beer since I still have a drive back."

Reese stood and held out his hand. "Thanks for everything, Stan."

Stan shook Reese's hand, his larger hand engulfing Reese's more delicate one.

"Don't mention it. Besides, if you thank me, I'll worry that you're going to fall off the face of the earth, never to be seen again."

Reese shook his head and watched as Stan took the remaining four beers with him and got into his truck. He turned down the drive and honked his horn as his lights disappeared from view.

Instead of heading back into the trailer, Reese returned to his lawn chair, relaxed, and watched as the stars came out around him.

The next day, Reese was repairing the broken hinge on the bathroom vanity when the phone rang. Setting his tools down, he walked over and picked it up.

"I saw the news all over the television," Millie Rae said.

Reese sat down at the kitchen table and put the phone between his ear and shoulder.

"It was a relief for me," Reese said. "How are you feeling about it?"

"Good," Millie Rae said. The line crackled a little. "I wish I could have seen the sentencing in person, but with my new classes I didn't want any association with the trial."

Reese nodded his head.

"Listen, Millie Rae, I'm buying a bike soon. It's nothing special, but maybe once I get comfortable on it, I can come into town sometime and we can try getting to know each other outside of Rouge Palace and everything that happened."

Millie Rae was silent on the other end of the line for a long time.

"I'd like that," she said, her voice thick. She cleared her throat. "It would mean a lot, Reese."

Reese tried to picture what she was doing, a sudden ache to see her welling up in him.

"You never know," he said. "It may be sooner rather than later. I do miss you, Millie Rae."

"Are you still comfortable out there? I can't imagine being so far away from everything. I think I'd go mad."

Reese smiled. "Yes, I'm comfortable. It's cheap to rent the land here, and since the trailer needed work, I didn't have to pay for much of it. I still need to find a job though."

"What would you like to try?"

"I'm hoping I can ask the guy I'm buying the bike from if he knows of anything. He runs the local convenience store, and he probably has a better idea than most where I might find work."

The line crackled again, and there was a comfortable silence between the two of them for a moment before Millie Rae spoke again.

"Well, whatever it is, you should try to enjoy it. You've had a rough go, Reese. I know it's not really tangible, but you should try to find something that makes you happy."

"I'm glad you're happy with teaching."

Millie Rae chuckled. "These kids have so much energy. I wonder if I ever had that much growing up, but it's fun to watch them, and you can tell the ones who really want to get better. They're constantly working at it."

"I should get going." Reese glanced at the clock above the door. "I think I'm going to try and buy that bike today."

"Good for you, Reese." There was a smile in her voice. "Don't be a stranger."

Reese hung up the line, the silence settling around him comfortably.

Reese made it to the convenience store by late afternoon. He felt giddy, like a kid at Christmas at the thought of being able to ride the bike back to the trailer. He knew it needed work, but he was crossing his fingers that the engine and tires were functional enough to do that.

He walked inside the store and nodded to Mart, who was ringing up a customer. Reese waited until the customer had left before walking up to the man.

"Good to see you back, Reese." Mart finished scribbling something on a piece of paper before looking up. "You ready to buy that bike?"

Reese reached into his billfold and pulled out the money. It was about a third of what he had left, but he set the money on the counter without hesitation. Mart counted it quickly before bending down and pulling out a stack of papers. Flipping through them, he set several on the counter.

"Now, this is the original license and title when I bought it. If you want to drive it on the road, you'll need plates. The owner's manual should be in the saddlebag. We can head outside and see what needs fixing before we sign the sale paperwork."

They went out the front, Mart flipping a sign on the door that said he would be back in five minutes. Around the back, they rolled the bike out into the open.

Reese knelt down and checked the tires.

"Do you think we can see if these will fill up?" Reese asked. "They'll need replacing, but just to get me back home."

They rolled the bike around to the front of the convenience store and up to the air pump. The tires filled quickly and despite their threadbare appearance, seemed to hold the air well enough.

"I haven't turned it on in a while. We may need to flush any fuel that's left and put new in to see if it'll truly start." Mart tapped the fuel gauge and opened the tank. "It honestly doesn't look like there's hardly any in there. Let's roll it over and fill it up and see if she starts."

Mart put a gallon in before getting on and putting the key in the ignition. Reese waited, his mouth tight as Mart turned the key. The bike coughed, then sputtered, shuddering as the engine turned over. Finally, black exhaust blew out the tailpipe, and the engine seemed to run smoothly.

Mart grinned at Reese.

"Let me drive it around the parking lot a couple times to see if she'll drive smoothly and then I'll let you have a turn."

Reese took a step back, and Mart pushed off the pavement. Mart took it in several slow circles, giving the engine time to adjust to being run again, before he accelerated and did one large lap before braking by the front of the store. The sound of the brakes squealing sounded like nails on a chalkboard, but the bike stopped.

Reese walked over as Mart put the kickstand down and got off. He gestured for Reese to get on and showed him where the clutch and brakes were. The old rubber of the handlebars was crumbling, and the loose pieces stuck to Reese's hand as he gripped them. Pulling up the kickstand, Reese walked the bike back and nodded to Mart as he pushed off and throttled the engine.

Reese felt the bike wobble at first, but he straightened it out, picking up speed as he became more comfortable. He took the bike around the parking lot twice before stopping next to Mart.

Reese cut the engine and got off.

"It's wonderful. It needs work like you said, but it's just what I needed." Reese grinned down at the bike. "You said I could stop by the garage to fix it up? What times are you there?"

Mart led him back into the store to finish the paperwork.

"I'm not there too often, but I've got a guy who shows up during normal business hours to look out for the place if anyone stops by. I'll just tell him to expect you."

They finished signing the paperwork, Reese putting everything into his backpack. Mart handed Reese the key. Reese gripped the key tight, promising himself he would make a lanyard or something so he wouldn't lose it.

"Thanks again, Mart. The bike will be great. And not walking here every time will save my feet, at least."

Mart waved him off.

"Glad to get it out of my hair. You ever need anything else, let me know."

Reese turned to leave, excited to drive the bike, but turned back.

"I need a job. Maybe if you hear of anything. I'm good with anything at this point. I'd just like to stay out here as long as I can."

Mart nodded.

"I'll keep you in mind. We take care of each other out here. I'm sure something will come up."

Reese wrote down the phone number at the trailer before waving goodbye and walking outside to his bike.

He got on, turned the ignition, and smiled as he pulled the bike out of the parking lot and onto the road. The cooling wind whipped by him as he drove. The drive back to the trailer took no time at all, and when he pulled up to the trailer and parked the bike, he looked down and traced the scars on his hand, knowing that that part of his life was behind him. He hadn't noticed it earlier, but he'd called the trailer home, and he realized that's what it was. It was a place no one could take from him, and maybe one day he could convince Millie Rae to come up and visit this place that was all his.